Paul Stewart is the very funny, very talented author of more than twenty books for children, including *The Edge Chronicles* and *Muddle Earth*, collaborations with Chris Riddell.

Chris Riddell is a well-known illustrator and political cartoonist. His work appears in the *Observer* and the *New Statesman*. He has illustrated many picture books and novels for young readers, including *Pirate Diary* by Richard Platt, which won the 2001 Kate Greenaway Medal.

Both live in Brighton, where they created *The Blobheads* together.

'Richly inventive and lucidly written' – *TES*

PAUL STEWART
& CHRIS RIDDELL

MACMILLAN CHILDREN'S BOOKS

Garglejuice, Silly Billy, Naughty Gnomes and *Purple Alert!* first published
individually in 2000 by Macmillan Children's Books

This omnibus edition published 2004 by Macmillan Children's Books
a division of Macmillan Publishers Limited
20 New Wharf Road, London N1 9RR
Basingstoke and Oxford
www.panmacmillan.com

Associated companies throughout the world

ISBN 0 330 43181 1

Text and illustrations copyright © Paul Stewart and Chris Riddell 2000

The right of Paul Stewart and Chris Riddell to be identified as the
authors of this work has been asserted by them in accordance
with the Copyright, Designs and Patents Act 1988.

1 3 5 7 9 8 6 4 2

A CIP catalogue record for this book is available from
the British Library.

Typeset by SX Composing DTP, Rayleigh, Essex
Printed and bound in Great Britain by Mackays of Chatham plc, Kent

GARGLEJUICE

P. S. For Joseph and Anna
C. R. For Katy

Chapter One

"You know your trouble," said Derek, shaking his blobby head gravely. "You don't get out enough."

Kevin the hamster tutted with irritation. "Of course I don't. That's because *I'm always locked inside this blooming cage*," he said loudly for Billy's benefit.

Billy put down his comic. "It's for your own good," he sighed. "You know what happened last time. That could have been a very nasty accident."

3

"*Hmmph*!" Kevin huffed. "Maybe I *wanted* to see the inside of the vacuum cleaner."

"Whatever," said Billy. "Don't let him out again, Derek." He frowned. "And put my baby brother down."

"Can't," said Derek. "I'm a dummy."

"You can say that again," snorted Kevin the hamster.

"No, I mean, I'm a *dummy*," said Derek. "Look! The High Emperor just loves chewing on my tentacle."

Sure enough, there was Silas chewing gummily on the Blobhead's tentacle, making soft cooing noises. Billy groaned. "As if my life isn't complicated enough already," he muttered.

It wasn't easy sharing a bedroom with three red and purple aliens who had arrived from the planet Blob,

convinced that Silas, Billy's baby brother, was the High Emperor of the universe – and matters had taken a definite turn for the worse when Derek taught his pet hamster to talk! Now, to crown it all, Silas was teething.

What with Silas's screaming and Kevin's constant chatter, Billy had been kept awake most of the previous night. And the night before that . . .

Just then, Kerek and Zerek burst into the room carrying a toothbrush and a tube of toothpaste.

"Is it here yet?" Kerek asked excitedly. "Has it arrived?"

"What?" said Billy.

"The High Emperor's first tooth, of course," said Kerek.

"Not yet," said Derek. He inspected his bruised tentacle. "But it won't be long now."

"Waaaah!" Silas screamed. He grabbed the tentacle, stuffed it back into his mouth and began chewing all the harder.

The three Blobheads beamed at him proudly.

"In that case, it won't be long before the High Emperor is invited to the dentist," said Kerek.

"That won't be for ages," said Billy.

"Though *I'm* going tomorrow."

The Blobheads turned on him in surprise.

"You have an invitation?" said Kerek. "*You?*"

"We didn't think you were important enough," said Zerek.

"Of course I am," said Billy. "Everyone's important enough to go to the dentist."

Clearly shocked by this latest piece of information, the three Blobheads huddled together, the blobs on their huge heads pulsing with red and purple light.

"What's the matter?" said Billy.

Kerek turned to face him. "The Great Computer clearly states that only the most important people are invited to dentists' parties."

"Parties?" said Billy.

"Come on, Billy," said Zerek. "We know all about dentists' parties. The fun. The games." He sighed dreamily. "And best of all, of course, the garglejuice!"

"Mmmm, garglejuice," the three Blobheads murmured, and licked their beaky lips.

"I don't know about that," said Billy. "*I* go to the dentist to make sure my

teeth are clean and healthy. He looks inside my mouth with a little mirror on a stick. Prods about a bit—"

"Yes, yes," said Zerek impatiently. "That's not important. You get garglejuice there, don't you? The Great Computer is quite clear on the matter . . ."

Billy frowned. It wasn't the first time that the Blobheads' so-called *Great* Computer had been wrong. "What is this garglejuice?" he said.

"What is *garglejuice*?" Zerek spluttered, unable to believe his listening-blobs. "It's only the most delicious drink in the known universe."

"Yum!" slurped Derek, his mouth watering.

"Garglejuice is so rare, so precious, it is only found on Earth at the place you call the dentist," said Kerek. "Scrumptiously refreshing, it is. A purple, perfumed mouthwash that—"

"Mouthwash?" said Billy surprised. "You mean the stuff you get when the dentist's finished looking at your teeth. The stuff you swill round your mouth and spit out."

The Blobheads started back in disbelief. Their blobs fizzed and buzzed.

"You spit it out!" said Kerek. "The nectar of the galaxy, and you spit it out! What an appalling waste!"

"Absolute madness!" Zerek agreed.

"I'd give my right tentacle if I could try garglejuice just once," said Derek, his mouth watering even more.

"Stop dribbling on my brother's head," said Billy.

"Sorry," said Derek. "Oh, but

garglejuice.   *Gaaaargle*juice!"   He
slurped noisily. "Billy, will you take me
to the dentist with you?"

"Typical," said Zerek. "Always
thinking of yourself."

"Will you take *all* of us?" asked
Kerek.

"No," said Billy.

"We promise to be good," said
Zerek. "Don't we?"

The three Blobheads nodded enthusiastically.

"No," said Billy.

"Please," said Derek.

"No!" said Billy.

"Pleeeease!" they all said together.

"Pretty please," added Kevin the hamster.

"NO!"

Chapter Two

The following afternoon, when he heard his dad beeping the horn outside, Billy grabbed the red and purple blobby hat, scarf and jacket and rushed downstairs. He didn't notice that the door to the hamster cage was ajar or that, for once, Kevin was silent.

As always, the Blobheads had morphed into everyday objects that they hoped would blend in. As always, they had got it wrong. It was a sunny day, yet Billy was dressed for the Arctic. When he climbed into the car, his dad looked at him curiously.

"What on earth are you wearing that lot for?" he said. "You must be sweltering."

Billy shrugged. "They wouldn't take no for an answer," he muttered.

Mr Barnes shook his head. "I've said

it before and I'll say it again: you are a strange boy, Billy Barnes."

Billy smiled. Better that his dad thought he was a bit weird than discover the truth about the Blobheads. "It's not that hot," he said.

"Not that hot?" said Mr Barnes. "It's *baking* . . . Speaking of which, I've got a treacle and Gorgonzola upside-down cake in the oven. If the traffic's bad in town, I'll drop you off at the corner. All right?"

"All right, Dad," said Billy.

"Mum'll pick you up at five."

Billy nodded.

The traffic *was* bad in town that afternoon and Billy had to complete his journey on foot. With Kerek disguised as the scarf, Zerek as the jacket and Derek a bobble hat, Billy was dripping with sweat by the time he reached the dentist's.

"Couldn't you have morphed into something a bit cooler?" said Billy crossly as he pushed the dentist's door open. He pulled the bobble hat from his head.

"How about this, then?" said Derek. Billy found himself holding a fluffy blue toy kangaroo. "Pretty cool, eh?"

Billy sighed. "Trust you!" he said. He shoved it under his arm. "Now, don't wriggle," he instructed. "And keep quiet."

"Quiet as a louse," said Derek.

"*Mouse*," Billy corrected him.

"Where?" said the scarf.

"Nowhere," said Billy.

"But—"

"As quiet as a mouse," he said. "That's what people say."

16

"But a mouse isn't quiet," said the jacket. "It squeaks . . ."

"Whereas a louse is always as silent as the gravy," said the fluffy blue toy kangaroo.

"Will you *all* be quiet!" Billy hissed. "If you can't be good, then I'm taking you back home right now!"

The three Blobheads fell silent. So close to tasting garglejuice for the very first time, they weren't about to mess up now.

"Thank you," Billy whispered. "Now stay quiet."

He walked into the reception area and looked around. There were five people waiting there. A teenager with a broken front tooth. A red-haired girl with her red-haired father. A bony old man who was making strange sucking noises. And a short portly woman with

17

a swollen jaw, who sat in the corner, moaning softly to herself.

Billy crossed the room to the reception desk.

"And you are?" said the receptionist, looking up.

"Billy Barnes."

The receptionist checked her lists. "Ah, good," she said. "One for Mr Wilberforce. If you were here to see Mrs Malone, you'd have a long wait."

At that moment, there was a loud *buzz* and the blue light on her desk flashed.

"Excellent," she said. "You can go straight up. Surgery 1."

The dental nurse – a young woman with flyaway hair and pink cheeks – greeted him at the door.

"Billy?" she said. Billy nodded.

"Come in, then."

Billy went inside.

"Afternoon," said Mr Wilberforce.

"Afternoon," said Billy.

"Now then," said the dental nurse. "We'll take off that scarf and jacket, shall we?"

Billy slipped them off, handed them over and glared at them severely as they were hung over the back of the chair by the door. For everyone's sake, he hoped that Kerek and Zerek would behave.

"And . . . errm. . ." the dental nurse continued, "shall I take the . . . erm . . . kangaroo, is it?"

"Yes, it is a kangaroo," said Billy. "And no, I'll keep hold of it, thanks."

"Come on now," she said, her cheeks getting pinker. "A big boy like you!"

She wrenched the fluffy blue toy kangaroo away. Derek squeaked uncomfortably.

"We'll put him over here on the table, so you'll still be able to see him."

"No!" said Billy insistently. "It really would be *much* better if I kept hold of him." He snatched him back. "Believe me!"

Mr Wilberforce nodded to his assistant that it was all right; he could hold onto his fluffy toy if he wanted.

"Nervous, are we?" he said.

"*I'm* not," said the kangaroo. "Just thirsty—"

Billy clamped his hand firmly round the kangaroo's nose. "Well, maybe a little nervous," he said.

Mr Wilberforce chuckled affably. "Well, there's nothing to be worried about." He nodded to his dental

nurse. "It's Miss Parfitt's first day here – she's probably more nervous than you! Jump up onto the chair. That's it. Now, open wide . . ."

Billy did as he was told. As Mr Wilberforce prodded about, the fluffy blue toy kangaroo noticed a movement out of the corner of his eye. It was the jacket and the scarf. They were sliding down off the back of the chair, slithering across to the door, slipping outside . . .

"Hey, you two," he cried out. "Wait for me!"

At least, that was what he *tried* to cry out. At the first sound he made, however, Billy squeezed his muzzle tightly shut. *"Unnh-unnh!"* Derek mumbled.

The dentist withdrew his mirror and prodder. "Sorry?" he said.

"Nothing," said Billy. "Just my tummy rumbling." He smiled. "I just wish it would KEEP QUIET!" he said. Derek squirmed about. "And STAY STILL!"

Mr Wilberforce glanced at his dental nurse and raised one eyebrow. Derek stopped moving.

"That's better," said Billy. He opened his mouth wide again.

The dentist continued with the check-up. The fluffy blue toy kangaroo remained absolutely still.

So far, so good, Billy thought.

Derek was transfixed. There, just out of reach, on a stand beside the reclining chair, was a glass of purple liquid. It was garglejuice!

And it was his, all his!

Outside on the landing, the scarf and jacket morphed back into Kerek and Zerek.

"That was boring!" said Kerek, shaking his blobby head.

"And not a drop of garglejuice to be seen," said Zerek. "Fine dentist *he* is!" He pointed to the door marked Surgery 2. "Let's try in there."

Slowly, cautiously, they crept across the landing. Below them, a buzzer sounded. Kerek reached up, pressed the handle and pushed the door. He peeked into the empty room.

"All clear," he whispered. "And look! *There's* the garglejuice." He nodded towards a large bottle of purple liquid on a shelf. "I—"

"Is that you, Mrs Gimble?" came a voice from the cupboard in the far corner of the room.

"That must be Mrs Malone," Kerek whispered. "The other dentist."

"I'll be right with you," she was saying. "I'm just trying to find your file."

The Blobheads went into the room. The dentist was standing in the doorway of the cupboard, her back turned.

"And you must excuse me for running so late this afternoon," she went on, as six little feet puttered across the tiles towards her. "My dental nurse fell ill earlier and I'm trying to carry on single-handed."

Six purple tentacle-arms rose up into the air.

"Do take a seat," she said.

Six purple tentacle-arms took her by the arms.

"What the . . . ?" Mrs Malone gasped.

Six purple tentacle-arms guided her gently, but firmly, into the cupboard. Zerek closed the door. Kerek turned the key in the lock.

"Alone at last!" he exclaimed. "Time for that garglejuice . . ."

There was a knock on the surgery door. Kerek and Zerek looked at each other.

"Who is it?" Kerek asked.

"It's Mrs Gimble," came the reply. "The receptionist told me to come up."

Zerek turned to Kerek. "What do we do now?"

Chapter Three

"Excellent," said Mr Wilberforce. His dental nurse made a note on the chart of Billy's teeth. "Absolutely nothing to worry about here."

Billy clamped his hands round the kangaroo snout tighter than ever. The dentist smiled.

"Relax, young man," he said. "Your teeth are fine. You've been taking excellent care of them. Now we'll just see how your molars are doing and then you can rinse out with some mouthwash."

Derek quivered in Billy's arms.

"Steady!" the dentist chuckled. "Soon be finished." He removed the mirror and prodder from Billy's mouth and turned to the dental nurse for a closer look at the chart.

The moment his back was turned Derek seized his chance. He reached out a fluffy blue paw towards the glass of purple mouthwash, and grasped it. Just then a small furry face appeared from his pouch.

"*Pfwoooah!*" Kevin exclaimed. "This pouch is worse than my cage!"

Miss Parfitt glanced round. "*Waaaaah!*" she screamed. Derek dropped the glass of mouthwash. It smashed on the tiled floor.

"A mouse!" shrieked Miss Parfitt.

"Miss Parfitt!" exclaimed the dentist.

"Kevin!" shouted Billy.

"Garglejuice!" wailed the blue kangaroo.

"Are you ready for me, then?" said Mrs Gimble from the landing outside Surgery 2.

"No . . . I mean, I don't know . . . I mean, yes," came a voice. It sounded flustered, and was followed by a lot of muffled bumping and clattering. "You'd better come in."

Mrs Gimble opened the door. She looked round uncertainly. There before her were two somewhat blobby figures in white coats. One of them was holding out a tray of drinks.

"Garglejuice?" he said.

Mrs Gimble didn't move. "You're not Mrs Malone," she said.

"No," the figure without the tray agreed. "But . . . we're dentists," he said eagerly. "I'm Mr Kerek. And this is Mr Zerek, my assistant. We were just having some garglejuice, if you'd care to join us."

"Why am *I* always *your* assistant?" said Zerek. "Why can't *you* be *my* assistant for once?"

"Be quiet, Zerek, and just pour the garglejuice!" said Kerek impatiently.

Zerek did as he was told, filling three glasses with the purple liquid. Kerek took one. Zerek took another.

"No thank you," said Mrs Gimble as Mr Zerek offered her the third.

"As you please," he said.

The two blobby dentists clinked their glasses together, cried "Blobs up!" and took a long, long slurp.

"Wow!" gasped Kerek.

"Deeeeee-licious," purred Zerek. "Go on," he said, shoving the tray under Mrs Gimble's nose. "Have some!"

"No, really, Mr Zerek, I—" Mrs Gimble began. From the cupboard, there came a low groaning noise.

"What was that?" she said.

"What was *what*?" said Kerek and Zerek together. They each took a second slurp of the garglejuice.

The noise came again, muffled and unclear – followed by a soft tapping sound.

"That!" said Mrs Gimble.

"Oh, *that*," said Kerek. "That's . . . *hic* . . . That's . . . Now, what are they called? Little furry things, scuttle around in corners, like cheese . . . *hic* . . ."

"Hamsters!" said Zerek.

"Hamsters?" said Mrs Gimble suspiciously.

"But never mind about them," said Kerek cheerily. He drained his glass, poured himself another and waved the bottle at Mrs Gimble. "Are you sure I can't tempt you?"

Mrs Gimble shook her head. "I don't want anything to drink," she said. "I just want you to do something about this terrible toothache."

"Oh, all right," said Kerek disappointedly. "Climb onto the chair, then."

Mrs Gimble sat down in the big dentist's chair. The tapping from the inside of the cupboard grew louder.

Kerek smiled. "Noisy little creatures, hamsters, aren't they? They're up half the night. They never stop talking." He had a slurp of garglejuice. "I sucked one up in a vacuum cleaner recently . . ."

But Mrs Gimble wasn't listening. "Aren't you going to recline the seat?" she said.

"Recline the seat?" said Kerek. "You mean, put the back of the seat down? Ah, yes, here we are."

He pressed a lever and hoped for the best. The seat abruptly tipped backwards. Mrs Gimble cried out and clutched at her throbbing tooth.

"Whoops!" said Kerek. "Bit *too* far." He pressed the lever a second time.

With a jolt, the backrest sprang upwards, catapulting Mrs Gimble forwards and launching her off the chair.

"Ooooh!" she squeaked as she tumbled forwards, and – THUD! – landed on the floor.

35

"*Waaaah!*" said Zerek, falling back against the wall in surprise. His blobby head bumped the buzzer-button.

Downstairs, the receptionist looked up. She saw the flashing red light on her desk.

"That was quick," she said to herself. "Still . . ." She looked down her list. "Mr Lewis," she said.

The bony old man looked up.

"If you'd like to go up, Mrs Malone will see you now."

Back in the surgery, Zerek was beside himself. "Blobby Heavens!" he exclaimed and hurried towards her. "Are you all right?"

Mrs Gimble moaned, her eyelids fluttered and she looked up dazed. "Is that you, Ethel?" she muttered.

"That's the spirit," said Kerek. "Now drink your garglejuice."

Across the landing in Surgery 1, Mr Wilberforce – down on all fours – was far from happy.

"You're a very silly boy, Billy," he said. "A fluffy toy's one thing, but bringing your pet is quite another." He turned to his dental nurse. "Miss Parfitt, please try to pull yourself together."

"A mouse!" sobbed Miss Parfitt, balancing unsteadily on top of her stool. "It could be anywhere! Find it!" she shrieked. "*Find it*!"

"That's exactly what we're trying to do," said Mr Wilberforce, as he reached underneath the reclining chair.

Billy was on his hands and knees over by the desk. "He's a hamster," he said, "not a mouse. Kevin. Kev-in!"

From the chair, the fluffy blue toy kangaroo looked down miserably at the broken glass and spilt garglejuice.

"It's all *her* fault," he muttered.

"Derek!" said Billy.

"Derek?" said Mr Wilberforce. "Did you say 'Derek'? I thought his name was Kevin. Just how many rodents *have* you brought with you?"

A ball of golden fur darted along

the skirting board between the table and the sink.

"There it is!" shouted Mr Wilberforce, lunging forwards. Billy skidded across the floor to head him off.

The fluffy blue toy kangaroo leant over and tapped Miss Parfitt on the leg. "I don't suppose there's any more garglejuice going?"

"*Waaaah*!" Miss Parfitt screamed as she tottered precariously on the stool. "Something soft and furry touched my leg and . . . Oh, help!" she cried, crashing to the floor.

Mr Wilberforce leapt to his feet. "Miss Parfitt!" he said. "Miss Parfitt, are you all right?"

Chapter Four

"It spoke to me," Miss Parfitt sobbed, her eyes darting anxiously all round the room. "It tapped me on the leg – and then spoke to me."

"There, there," said Mr Wilberforce, patting her hand awkwardly.

"It *did*," she said, sitting up. "I heard it. It wants . . . garglejuice."

"Of course it does," said Mr Wilberforce soothingly.

Billy seized the fluffy blue toy kangaroo by the paw and peered round the room. The longer Kevin the hamster remained missing, the more convinced Billy became that he was up to something.

"You're just a little overwrought," Mr Wilberforce said as he helped the flustered dental nurse to her feet.

"But I did feel something," Miss Parfitt said.

"I'm sure you did," said Mr Wilberforce.

"Oh, and look!" said Miss Parfitt, bursting into tears. "The patients' notes are all over the floor."

"Never mind," said Mr Wilberforce.

"But I so wanted everything to run smoothly," she sobbed. "Today of all days."

The dentist chuckled. "I remember *my* first day," he said. "I was so nervous,

I could barely drill straight."

Miss Parfitt smiled bravely.

"Come on, now," said Mr Wilberforce. "I'll give you a hand."

Mr Wilberforce collected up the pieces of paper and, still shaking, Miss Parfitt attempted to get them into some sort of order.

On the other side of the room, Kevin the hamster finally found what he was looking for.

"*Psssst*, Derek!" he hissed.

Billy and the fluffy blue toy kangaroo looked up. Kevin was up on the shelf by the open window, leaning nonchalantly against a five-litre container of purple mouthwash with one paw, the plastic screw-on top in the other.

"Yes!" Derek exclaimed. He wriggled out of Billy's grasp and bounced

towards the shelf. "Garglejuice, here I come!"

Mr Lewis walked into Surgery 2.

"It's my dentures," he said. "They're just not right. They don't fit properly."

He stopped. His mouth fell open.

Two blobby dentists and the woman he'd noticed earlier in the waiting room were clustered together by the cupboard in the corner. The dentists seemed to be helping the woman to her feet, totally unaware that he had entered the room.

"What do you mean you don't want any garglejuice?" one of them was saying. "How can you resist?"

"I just don't," the woman snapped.

"Very peculiar, Mr Zerek," he said. "She doesn't seem to like garglejuice."

"All the more for us then, Mr Kerek," replied the other. "It's *so* delicious." He looked up and saw Mr Lewis. "Oops . . . *hic*," he said. "Here's another one."

Mr Lewis frowned. "What's going on?" he said. A muffled hammering came from the cupboard. "And what's that noise?"

Zerek sighed with exasperation. "Oh, not you as well. We've already

45

explained that. *Hic.* Hamsters."

"And I'm telling you, you mean *mice* not *hamsters,*" said Mrs Gimble.

"You're wrong," said Kerek. "Mice squeak. Hamsters speak. *Hic.* It's a well-known fact."

"Anyway, it doesn't sound like mice to me at all," Mrs Gimble persisted. "It sounds like someone's locked inside!"

"The very idea!" Zerek groaned as he struggled to pick Mrs Gimble up from the floor. "*Hic.* I . . . *unnkh*!" he grunted as he stumbled against the wall. His blobby head bumped the buzzer-button.

Down in the waiting room, the receptionist frowned. "Most peculiar," she said. She looked up at the teenager with the broken front tooth. "Vincent James," she said. "Mrs Malone will see you now."

"Oh, no," he groaned.

Back upstairs, Kerek turned to Mr Lewis and stumbled forwards. He raised the half-full bottle of purple liquid. "Garglejuice," he announced loudly. "Nectar of the universe—"

"Let me out!" came a muffled voice from the cupboard.

Mr Lewis backed away, open-mouthed, and groped for the door. At that moment there was a knock. The door opened and Vincent James blundered in, head down, hands in pockets – and, *boof*, walked straight into Mr Lewis.

The sudden jolt sent his ill-fitting false teeth leaping from his open mouth. They soared across the room.

"Well I never!" exclaimed Kerek.

"*Waaaaah*! He's falling to bits!" shouted Zerek, staggering back. His

47

blobby head bumped the buzzer-
button for the third time.

"Good grief," the receptionist
muttered to herself. "Mrs Malone's
certainly getting through them today!
Mr Blevins," she said. "If you'd like to
take Belinda up now."

Billy had Derek by the tail. "Come
here!" he shouted.

At the same moment, Mr Wilberforce spotted Kevin the hamster on the shelf.

"You won't get away this time!" he roared.

Miss Parfitt dropped her bundle of papers and scrambled back onto the stool. Mr Wilberforce lunged, made a grab for the hamster – and tripped over Billy.

CRASH!

The container of mouthwash wobbled from side to side, before toppling over by the open window. Derek watched in horror as the rare and precious, scrumptiously refreshing, purple, perfumed garglejuice gushed out of the five-litre container and down onto the street below.

"NO!" he wailed.

*

"I'm really sorry," said Vincent James. "I never look where I'm going."

"By benpures," Mr Lewis wailed gummily, as he crawled around the floor. "Pind by benpures!"

The hammering on the cupboard door grew louder, and the voice more insistent than ever. "LET ME OUT OF HERE!"

"I *knew* there was someone in there," said Mrs Gimble, tugging at the cupboard door.

"Honestly!" said Mr Zerek, reclining lazily in the dentist's chair. He took another large slurp of garglejuice. "It's nothing. Just hampers," he slurred. "I mean, *hamsters*. Tha'sall . . ."

The door to the surgery opened again and Mr Blevins came in, with Belinda trailing reluctantly behind him.

"They just keep on coming," Kerek laughed jovially, and staggered towards them. "Garglejuice all round?" he said.

At that moment, behind them, the lock gave way and the cupboard door flew open. Mrs Malone stumbled out, red-faced and dishevelled. She bumped into Mr Blevins and Belinda.

"What on earth is going on?" she yelled.

"We've only just got here," said Mr Blevins. "Haven't we, Belinda?"

Belinda burst into tears.

"So have I," agreed Vincent James.

"It was those *other* dentists," Mrs Gimble insisted.

"*What* other dentists?" Mrs Malone demanded.

"The blobby ones," said Mrs Gimble. "Mr Kerek and Mr Zerek—"

"WHO?" bellowed Mrs Malone.

They all looked around. There was a red and purple blobby scarf lying across the dentist's chair; a red and purple blobby jacket over the door. But of the two dentists, not a trace.

From the corner of the room came a plaintive voice. It was Mr Lewis. "Who trod on my benpures?" he said.

No one in Surgery 1 noticed the door opening, nor saw the scarf and jacket slipping quietly through the narrow gap.

Billy was standing over by the dentist's chair, with Kevin the hamster in one hand and Derek the fluffy blue toy kangaroo in the other. He was ready to go.

"Don't forget your jacket and scarf," said Mr Wilberforce. "Oh, dear," he said. "They must have slipped off the chair." He brushed them down and hung them over Billy's arm.

"Thanks," said Billy. At least *two* of the Blobheads had been behaving themselves.

"Now remember, hamsters belong in cages not dentist surgeries," Mr Wilberforce was saying. "Still, cute little fellow . . ." His voice trailed off as he noticed his dental nurse pulling off her green dental coat. "Miss Parfitt?" he said.

"I resign!" she announced.

"I'll be off, then," said Billy, slipping out of the door before Mr Wilberforce decided to blame him for losing his new assistant.

"*Hic.*"

Pausing only briefly to listen to the clamour of voices coming from Surgery 2, Billy made his way to the

top of the stairs. There, he slipped his jacket on, stuffed Derek and Kevin in the pockets and hung the scarf around his neck.

"*Hic.*"

Billy frowned and looked round. "Is that you, Kerek?"

"No – *hic* – it's me, Zerek," said the jacket. From the scarf came the sound of soft snoring. Zerek giggled. "Kerek's asleep. It must have been all the excitement," he yawned.

"Hmmph!" said Billy, as he set off down the stairs. If the Blobheads had been bored, they only had themselves to blame. He'd told them not to come.

The waiting room was all but empty. Mrs Barnes looked up from the bench opposite.

"Hello, Mum," said Billy. "The dentist says my teeth are fine and . . ." He paused. "Mum?"

"Yes, Billy?"

"You're soaking wet!"

"I know I'm soaking wet," she said crossly. "Just as I was walking in through the door I got drenched! Some clot was pouring mouthwash out of an upstairs window!"

Billy frowned guiltily. "Someone's

57

idea of a joke," he said.

"Yes, well," said Mrs Barnes, throwing a furious glance at the receptionist. "I don't think it's funny. Come on, Billy, let's go home."

No one spoke on the journey back. Mrs Barnes was wondering how she would ever get the purple stain out of her suit. Billy was wondering whether the school jumble sale would accept a hamster and a toy kangaroo. And Kevin the hamster was wondering whether he'd ever be allowed out of his cage again.

The only noise to be heard was the soft, slurpy sound of a fluffy blue toy kangaroo sucking on the hem of a soggy jacket.

It wasn't until bedtime, when the Blobheads had morphed back and the hamster was in his cage once more, that Billy had a chance to tell Derek and Kevin exactly what he thought of their behaviour.

"I mean, why couldn't you have been like Kerek and Zerek?" he said. "*They* were good."

"No they weren't," said Derek. "I saw them—"

"Derek!" said Zerek sharply. "Don't

make matters worse by telling lies."

"But I did see them!" said Derek, waving his tentacles about agitatedly.

"*Waaaah!*" screamed Silas indignantly, as the comforting tentacle abruptly disappeared from his mouth.

Derek plugged it back in.

"Anyway," said Billy. "That's the last time I take you lot to the dentist's."

"Spoilsport," Kevin the hamster muttered sulkily from his cage.

"And as for *you!*" said Billy. "You're grounded! Another word out of you and you'll be the prize exhibit on the white elephant stall at the school jumble sale."

"My lips are sealed," said Kevin innocently. "And now, if you'll excuse me, I've got a thrilling appointment with a hamster wheel." He sighed. "Will the excitement never end?"

At that moment, Derek let out a yelp and yanked his tentacle from Silas's mouth.

"That hurt!" he said.

"Wonderful news!" said Kerek. "The High Emperor's first tooth has arrived."

Silas looked up and grinned. One small, shiny white tooth was poking up

from the gum.

"Now we'll *have* to go back to the dentist's again!" said Zerek.

"Oh, no you won't!" said Billy. "And this time, when I say 'no', I mean 'no'. Absolutely not. No, no, no! Not in a month of Sundays. Never, ever . . ."

But the Blobheads weren't listening. Blobby heads pulsing with red and purple light, they opened their mouths and uttered one single word together.

"*Garglejuice!*"

SILLY BILLY

P. S. For Anna and Joseph
C. R. For Jack

Chapter One

"And where do you think you're going, Billy?" said Mr Barnes as he caught sight of his older son hurrying past the open kitchen door. He pushed another spoonful of pumpkin and passion-fruit fool into baby Silas's mouth. "Billy?"

"Yummy-gummy," gurgled a very gooey Silas, happily spitting it out on to the floor.

Billy stopped and poked his head round the door. "Over to Simon's," he said. "He's got a new computer game. *Splat Attack 2*. And he promised I could have a go."

Mr Barnes looked up and frowned. "*Splat Attack*?" he said, dripping more of the glistening gloop on to Silas's head. "What's that all about?"

"It's really cool, Dad," said Billy. "You've got to save the earth from hordes of aliens hurling purple pies."

"Aliens hurling purple pies?" said Mr Barnes. "How ridiculous."

"Oh, I don't know," said Billy. "It's not as ridiculous as you might think!"

If his dad thought *they* were ridiculous, then he should see the three aliens who lived up in Billy's bedroom. Now they *were* ridiculous. They had arrived out of the blue – or rather, out of the toilet – in search of the High Emperor of the Universe who was, according to their so-called Great Computer, none other than Billy's baby brother, Silas.

Mr Barnes wiped Silas's head with a damp sponge. "Anyway," he said. "You're not playing any games this afternoon. You promised Mrs Turbot that you'd deliver those leaflets for the school fair."

"Oh, but—" Billy protested.

"And you still haven't washed Mr Arkwright's car, even though he gave you a pound last week to do it."

"Yes, but I—"

"And don't forget Mrs Ramsden's lawn. You promised to mow it for her ages ago."

Billy sighed.

"And before any of that, I want you to go and tidy your room," Mr Barnes continued, without taking a breath. "It's an absolute tip!"

"Oh, Da-ad," Billy complained.

"Now!" said Mr Barnes.

"Goo, goo, goo," Silas burbled contentedly as Billy stomped up the stairs.

Mr Barnes called up after him. "And don't slam your bedroom door—"

SLAM!

*

"I do wish you wouldn't bang the door like that," said the spotty red and purple rubber ring.

"Yes," said the striped red and purple beach ball irritably. "Why do you always have to be so loud?"

"You made me jump," complained the giant fluffy pink elephant.

"Oh, be quiet, the lot of you!" said Billy, flinging himself on the bed. "No

wonder my dad thinks the bedroom's messy, with you lot cluttering up the place in your ridiculous disguises," he said, eyeing the elephant furiously.

The rubber ring, the beach ball and the elephant morphed back into the three Blobheads: Kerek, Zerek and Derek.

"A giant fluffy pink elephant!" said Billy. "I mean, honestly!"

"Yes," said Zerek irritably. "You're meant to blend in with your surroundings when you morph."

"I was trying to turn myself into a watering can," Derek explained sheepishly. "But it all went a bit wrong—"

"You get everything wrong!" snapped Kerek.

"I don't know why the Great Computer insisted on us bringing him along in the first place," said Zerek. "He's been nothing but trouble from the moment we—"

"For heaven's sake, shut up!" Billy shouted. "All of you!"

"Dear, dear," said Kevin the hamster. "Who rattled *his* cage?"

Billy sighed. Not only could Derek never morph into anything sensible, but he'd also taught Billy's pet hamster to talk. Now it was difficult to persuade Kevin to be quiet. Billy might have known that he would stick his oar in.

"Yeah, who ruffled his fur?" said Kevin the hamster, turning to Kevin the hamster. "That's what I want to know."

"Search me," said a third Kevin the hamster. "Do *you* know why he's in such a bad mood?"

"No idea," said the fourth Kevin the hamster. "He was born grumpy if you ask me."

"Hang on a minute," Billy muttered. He jumped off the bed, rushed over to the cage and peered in. "Oh, what?" he exclaimed.

Kevin was reclining on a soft bed of crumpled tissue paper, surrounded by three other hamsters, identical to him

in every way. One of them was grooming his fur. One was polishing his nails. A third was delicately peeling him a grape.

"This is the life," he sighed.

"What on earth's going on?" Billy demanded. "When I went downstairs there was just one of you."

"They're my three little helpers," said Kevin. "Aren't you?"

The three attendant hamsters nodded solemnly.

Billy spun round and glared at Derek. "You've been using that Megawotsit Multi-Thingy Gizmo of yours again, haven't you?"

Derek shrugged. "Might have," he said. "But there's no harm done," he added. "And anyway, Kevin asked me to. Insisted! Said he was lonely; said he needed a bit of company."

"But how could you?" said Billy.

"Oh, it was easy," said Derek. "I just pressed the button and—"

"That's not what I mean!" Billy interrupted him. "The last time you used it I found forty-six Silases in the bedroom. And what a mess that was!"

"That was a mistake," said Derek. "It's working perfectly now – and all you have to do to reverse it is press this button here." He pointed the gizmo at the cage and pressed three times.

Zap. Zap. Zap.

Kevin's three helpers disappeared.

"Oi!" shouted Kevin the hamster indignantly. "I was enjoying that!"

"Well, I'm sorry, Kevin," said Billy, "but you'll just have to peel your own grapes!"

"But it's not fair!" Kevin complained.

"Life's not fair!" said Billy grumpily. "I've got to deliver Mrs Turbot's leaflets, wash Mr Arkwright's car, mow Mrs Ramsden's lawn – *and* tidy up the mess in here!"

Kerek stepped forwards. "It sounds like *you* could do with a little helper," he said.

"No!" said Billy.

"All your chores would be done for you," said Zerek.

"No," said Billy. "Absolutely not."

"But it's as easy as cake," said Derek. "And you've just seen how simple it is to reverse it."

"All the same," said Billy, a little less certainly.

"You'll have time to put your feet up," said Kerek, "and—"

"And go and play on my friend Simon's computer game," said Billy. "Hmmm. When you put it like that . . ." He nodded. "OK, then. But nothing had better go wrong."

"Nothing will," said Kerek.

"Have a little faith," said Zerek.

Derek raised the gizmo and pointed it at Billy.

Billy swallowed. "Why have I got the horrible feeling that I'm going to live to regret this," he muttered.

Derek pressed the button. There was a dazzling flash of light and an odd *boing*! "Hmm, it's never done that before," said Derek. "Still, never mind."

Chapter Two

Billy crept down the stairs, along the hall and out through the front door. The catch clicked softly in the lock.

Mr Barnes frowned. He looked at his wife. "Was that Billy going out?" he said. "I distinctly told him that he couldn't go round to Simon's." He jumped up from the table, strode crossly into the hall and shouted upstairs.

"Billy? Billy, are you up there?"

Billy appeared at the top of the

stairs and beamed down at him vacantly. "Yes, Father?" he said.

"I . . . errm. Nothing, Billy. Just . . . I could have sworn . . ." He nodded seriously. "How's that bedroom coming along? I hope it's looking a bit tidier."

Billy giggled. "As tidy as a tadpole," he said.

Mr Barnes sighed. "Stop being silly,

Billy." He pulled Mrs Turbot's box of school-fair leaflets out from under the stairs and picked it up. "Just go and deliver these leaflets."

Billy nodded and marched down the stairs. "Your wish is my umbrella," he announced as he slipped the box under his arm and headed for the front door.

"And try not to take all day!"

"As quick as a panda – and twice as smelly. That's me!" said Billy brightly.

Mr Barnes frowned. "And when you've done the leaflets, there's Mr Arkwright's car and Mrs Ramsden's lawn," he said. "Don't forget!"

Billy opened the door.

"And don't slam the—"

SLAM!

Mr Barnes returned to the kitchen. "Was it my imagination?" he said to his wife, "or was Billy behaving even more strangely than usual?"

At the first door he came to, Billy stopped, removed a leaflet from the box and neatly tore it in half. Then in half again. And again, and again, and again . . .

"Greetings, porcupines!" he cried out as he tossed the handful of

confetti into the air. "And may your vegetables all explode with joy!'

It was the same story at the next house. And the one after that. And the one after that. Both sides of the road, he did; four roads in all, until all the leaflets were gone. Then, chortling happily, he placed the empty box on his head.

"My herrings have wings," he trilled as he skipped off to carry out his second chore.

Mr Arkwright's dirty blue car was parked in the drive next to the house. There was a note under the windscreen.

Dear Billy, it said. *Thank you for coming! You'll find everything you need in the kitchen.* And it was signed. *W. W. Arkwright.*

Billy made his way round to the back of the house. There was a bucket and sponge on the mat. There was a bottle of tomato ketchup on the shelf, a can of whipped cream by the fridge, a packet of Rich Tea biscuits beside the kettle. Billy took them all. He marched back to the car.

"My gravy is lumpy and my custard is blue," Billy sang tunelessly as he dolloped the ketchup and squirted the foaming whipped cream all over the car and rubbed it around with the sponge.

Then, ripping open the packet of Rich Tea, Billy pulled out two biscuits at a time, scrunched them up in his hands and tossed them at the car. Handful after handful, he threw – at the windscreen, the headlamps, the hubcaps.

"Ooh, doctor, is that a grapefruit behind your ear?" he chirruped happily. "Ding-dong! The frogs go bong! May-day, may-day!"

Finally, he stood back, folded his arms and looked at the car admiringly.

"Frib-frib!" he exclaimed and dashed off to complete his final chore.

"Ah, Billy," said Mrs Ramsden when

Billy's grinning face appeared at her kitchen window. "Have you come to do my lawn for me? You are a good boy."

She dried her hands on the tea towel and bustled outside.

"Did you know you've got a cardboard box on your head, dear?" she said.

"Avast there, me hearties!" Billy cried and covered one eye with his hand as a pretend eyepatch.

"Oh, I see," said Mrs Ramsden, smiling uncertainly. "I've got a pirate to mow my lawn for me today, have I?" She opened the shed and pulled out the rotary mower. "You've used it before, so you know what to do," she said. "But remember, always keep the flex behind you."

Billy nodded. "Your hula hoop is my

command," he muttered gleefully.

Mrs Ramsden frowned. "There we are then, dear," she said as she plugged it in. "I'll go and see about a nice glass of iced lemonade."

Billy chuckled happily as he flicked the switch. The lawnmower whirred into action.

"Mountains of yoghurt and oceans of jam," he cried out as he swept the mower through the long grass cutting first one wide arc, then a second, and then a long line between the two, until the first of three letters appeared.

B

"Come on in, the baked beans are lovely!" Billy yodelled, as a long sweeping curve of the mower resulted in the second letter.

U

"A turnip has kidnapped my tortoise!"

Up and down, he mowed. Up and down. The third letter appeared.

M

Chapter Three

It was four o'clock when Billy made his way home. He hadn't enjoyed Simon's new game that much. It wasn't a patch on the original *Splat Attack*.

As he turned into Beech Avenue, he noticed the thick sprinkling of confetti all over the doormat of number 2.

"Odd," thought Billy.

When he saw a similar pile at number 4, he frowned. At number 6, he paused and scratched his head. At number 8, he could hide his curiosity no longer. He walked up the path, crouched and picked up one of the scraps of paper. There was printed writing on one side.

SCHOOL FA— it said.

"Uh-oh!" Billy groaned.

Quickening his step, Billy hurried along towards number 32, where he lived. Each house he passed had the same pile of confetti on its doorstep, while more of the stuff was blowing out from the gardens opposite.

"Oh, no," he groaned. He was beginning to panic now.

Then he saw a car – the blue car that Mr Arkwright was so proud of. It wasn't blue now. It was red and white, covered in a thick dripping gloop and studded with biscuit crumbs.

Billy froze. His jaw dropped. His

heart pounded. Things were even worse than he'd imagined.

Running now, he hurried home and dashed round the back of the house. Then, scarcely daring to look, he pulled himself up on the fence and peered over into Mrs Ramsden's garden. He saw the three huge letters mown into the long grass.

"Oh my goodness!" he exclaimed.

Billy raced upstairs and burst into his bedroom. A fluffy elephant, a rubber ring and a beach ball looked up calmly.

"We knew it was you," said Kerek. "You're *so* noisy."

"What on earth's been going on?" Billy shouted.

"Well," said Derek, smiling. "Zerek's been showing me something clever

you can do with an elephant and a
rubber ring, and—"

"And how many times do I have to
tell you?" said Zerek impatiently. "It
won't work if you bend your trunk!"

Billy shook his head impatiently. "I
don't mean you lot," he said. "What's
Billy been up to?"

There was silence as the blobby toys
morphed back into Blobheads.

Kerek frowned. "I thought you were going to play with that friend of yours, what's his name?"

"Susan," said Derek.

"Simon," said Billy. "But I don't mean me-Billy. I mean the other one. The other Billy."

"Oh, him!" said Zerek. "He's out doing your chores."

"Doing chores?" said Billy. "He's gone mad!"

"What, madder than you?" said Kevin the hamster. "That's hard to imagine."

"He's torn every single one of Mrs Turbot's leaflets into a hundred pieces," Billy said. "He's covered Mr Arkwright's car with ketchup and broken biscuits. And you wouldn't believe what he's done to Mrs Ramsden's lawn!"

Kerek, Zerek and Derek huddled together. Their pulsing red and purple blobs fizzed and buzzed.

"Curious," said Kerek at last.

"Very odd," said Zerek.

"What?" said Billy.

Derek pulled the gizmo from his belt and inspected it closely. "I'm sure I didn't break the wizzometer. Perhaps the jambles are a bit dirty."

"It's more likely to be a problem with your digital loops," said Kerek.

"Unless your oscillating flange is on the blink," said Zerek.

Kerek took the small black box from Derek and shook it. Something rattled inside. "Then again," he said, "with this model, replication is never going to be an exact science."

"Not an exact science!" Billy exclaimed loudly.

"Is that you, Billy?" a voice floated up from downstairs. It was Mr Barnes.

"Yes, Dad," Billy called back.

"You're back earlier than I thought. Dinner'll be about another half hour. Sausage and syrup casserole, and chocolate-chip onion ice cream for afters. I expect you're hungry."

Billy groaned. The smell of meat and toffee floated up the stairs. "Not *that* hungry, Dad," he said, wishing for the thousandth time that his gourmet dad would simply open a box of fish fingers for a change.

"You will be," said his dad confidently. "Anyway, better get back to my sauce. And thanks again for taking Silas to the park. I hope you both had fun."

Billy's bedroom fell completely still as Mr Barnes's words sank in. Billy looked at the Blobheads. The Blobheads looked at one another.

"Oh, no," said Billy.

"Oh, no," said the Blobheads.

"Oh, yes!" said Kevin the hamster.

"You don't think?" said Kerek, pulling the Great Computer from his belt and stabbing at the buttons.

"Not with Silas," said Derek, his blobby head wobbling with distress.

"*Waaaaaah!*" screamed Zerek. His purple and red blobs flashed on and off. "Purple alert! Purple alert!" he shrieked. "Don't panic! Mad, crazy, silly Billy has abducted the High Emperor of the Universe. *Waaaaaaah!*"

"Control yourself, Zerek!" Kerek commanded.

"Yes, pull yourself to pieces," said Derek.

"Together!" Billy corrected him.

"Pull yourself to pieces!" all three Blobheads chanted in unison.

"Our first duty is to maintain the safety of the Most High Emperor of the Universe," said Kerek.

"We have been neglectful in that duty," said Zerek. "Now we must make amends. We must find this silly Billy and zap him back to whence he came."

"Blobheads to the rescue!" Derek cried.

Chapter Four

Billy never liked going out with the Blobheads, but on this occasion even he could see that there was no choice. His baby brother was in the clutches of a loony version of himself – a Billy so silly it had already messed up all the chores it had been given. What would it do with Silas? Smear *him* all over with tomato ketchup? Tear *him* into tiny little pieces? Give him a haircut? It didn't bear thinking about.

"Are you ready?" he asked the Blobheads.

"Ready and willing," said the red and purple blobby skateboard.

"Is that you, Kerek?" said Billy.

"It is," said the skateboard. "Zerek's the jacket."

"As always," the blobby jacket complained. "I don't know why I always have to be. I'd far rather be something with wheels . . ."

"Guess who!" said the helmet. "It's me. Derek."

Billy looked at the heavy metal Viking helmet with curved and pointed horns. "I'd never have guessed," he muttered. "Come on, then. Let's go."

With the jacket over his shoulder, the helmet on his head and the skateboard under his arm, Billy made for the door.

"Wait a minute," said Kerek. "Where's the gizmo?"

"I thought you had it," said Zerek. "Derek?"

Derek shook his blobby head. "I haven't got it," he said.

"Well someone must have!" said Billy. "It can't just have disappeared." He frowned. "Can it?"

There was a jangle and rattle as a tiny paw tried to pull the black gizmo in through the bars of the cage.

"Kevin!" shouted Billy. "What are you doing with that?"

"I wanted my little helpers back," said Kevin the hamster.

"Give it to me at once!" said Billy.

"Ask nicely."

Billy snatched it away and dashed off. The bedroom door slammed.

"Charming!" said Kevin huffily.

Billy was at the top of the stairs when the knock came on the front door. He hesitated. Mr Barnes emerged from the kitchen and opened it.

"Look at this!" came an angry voice. It was Mrs Turbot. She let a handful of the confetti flutter down on to the carpet. "My leaflets!" she said. "He's done this to each and every one of them."

"Uh-oh," Billy muttered.

"Just go!" said the skateboard urgently.

"All right," said Billy. He raced down the stairs.

"There he is!" said Mrs Turbot.

Mr Barnes turned. "Slow down a minute, young man," he said. Billy ran past him. "Billy, I want a word with you—"

"Sorry, Dad, Mrs Turbot," said Billy

hurriedly. "Can't stop. It's a matter of life and death."

And with that, he leaped down the steps and on to the garden path. Mr Arkwright appeared at the other end. His face was purple with rage.

"What on earth do you think you've been playing at?" he roared.

"Is there a problem?" Mr Barnes called. "Didn't Billy clean your car properly?"

"Clean it properly?" Mr Arkwright blustered. "He's turned it into a giant trifle!"

"A what?" said Mr Barnes.

"I can explain," said Billy. He dropped the skateboard on to the path and jumped on. "But not now," he said, as he sped past Mr Arkwright and out on to the pavement.

Mrs Ramsden's head appeared

above the fence. She looked troubled. "I know I should be grateful for the extra help," she said. "But . . . but . . ." She burst into tears. "There's an enormous B-U-M on my lawn!'

"Whoooah!" Billy exclaimed and flapped his arms about wildly as the skateboard hurtled across the road, skidded round the corner and flew through the park gates. It was half-past six and, apart from an old man walking his whippet, the park was deserted.

"Where are they?" Billy asked, his heart thumping wildly. "Where have they gone?"

He jumped from the skateboard, picked it up and ran across the grass in the direction of the playground. There was no one playing football on the pitches he crossed, no one playing tennis on the courts he passed – and as he approached the playground, that too looked empty.

The swings were hanging motionless; the roundabout was still. Then a voice broke the silence.

"Rejoice! Rejoice! My budgie lies over the ocean and the gerbils are all running free!"

"There!" screamed the skateboard.

"At the top of the slide!" yelled the jacket.

Billy looked up. And there, seated at the very top with his legs on the steps and a cardboard box on his head, was the spitting image of himself. It was like looking in a mirror – apart, of course, from the cardboard box.

The other Billy waved. "Waiter, waiter, there's a hippopotamus in my soup!" he cried.

"Where's my baby brother, Silas?" Billy shouted up.

His double looked down and grinned. "My bubble and squeak is burned to a crisp!" he announced happily.

"This is hopeless," said Billy. "I'm coming up there."

Taking the steps two at a time, Billy bounded up to the top of the slide. As he arrived, the other Billy pushed himself off.

"Wheeee!" he cried. "The boats are full of treacle!"

Billy watched him sliding down and landing on the ground with a bump. His baby brother was not with him.

"Silas!" he shouted, scanning all round the park. "*Silas!*"

"Blobber-blobber, goo!" came a tiny voice from behind him.

Billy spun round and looked down. And there was Silas, sitting in the sandpit, waving his spade in the air.

"Silas!" Billy exclaimed.

"High Emperor of the Universe!" shouted the jacket.

"Thank Blob!" muttered the helmet.

Billy flew down the slide, dashed to the sandpit and picked Silas up in his arms. "Oh, Silas," he gasped. "You're safe now!"

"Blobberlob!" Silas gurgled.

"Yes, it's me," said Billy, hugging him tightly.

Silas twisted round and pointed a podgy finger at the figure with the

cardboard box on his head now sitting at one end of the see-saw.

"One hump or two?" it was shouting.

"Billa-blobber-lob!" said Silas and giggled.

"No, Silas," said Billy. "*I'm* the real Billy. That's . . . that's Silly Billy."

Silas's face creased up into a smile. "Blibby-slibby."

"But not for much longer," the skateboard announced. "Billy, zap the impostor!"

Billy nodded and placed Silas gently on the ground. He raised the gizmo. He lined up his double in the sights. Then, with a trembling finger, he pressed the button.

ZAP!

There was a loud bang and a blinding flash and . . .

"OH, NO!" Billy screamed.

The playground was suddenly full. There were three boys on each of the swings, a dozen on the slide, twenty on the roundabout, countless more in the sandpit, on the field, up the trees – and every one a copy, not of Billy – but of Silly Billy. The noise was deafening.

"My piano is in need of a cheese and pickle sandwich!" cried one.

"You must take two rhinos four times a day," cried another.

And a chorus of "Purple pie! Purple pie! We want purple pie!" echoed from the sandpit.

"You pressed the wrong button!" the helmet shouted.

"I didn't," Billy shouted back. "The gizmo must have malfunctioned."

"My nose is a tulip. My nose is a tulip."

"The doughnuts are wearing silk pyjamas!"

"But only when there's an eel in the month—"

"DO SOMETHING!" Billy roared.

Without saying a word, the skateboard morphed back into Kerek. He grabbed the gizmo and stabbed frantically at the buttons.

"You're right," he muttered. "It has malfunctioned. I think the nether-sprockets might be broken." He opened the back, pulled a buzzing screwdriver from his belt and poked about inside.

All around him, the multitude of Silly Billies were running amok, jumping, jostling and gurgling with joy.

"My parrots are inconvenient!"

"Saddle up the poodle!"

"Tickle the walrus!"

"Hurry *up!*" said Billy urgently. His countless doubles were getting increasingly overexcited.

"Nearly done," said Kerek. He clicked the back of the gizmo shut. "Everyone *not* a Silly Billy get behind me, now!" he bellowed.

Billy grabbed Silas, held him in his arms and ran back. He checked that he was still wearing the jacket and helmet. "Ready," he said.

"Right," said Kerek grimly. He raised the gizmo and set the co-ordinates to wide-angle. The tip of his tentacle hovered over the button. "Here goes," he muttered.

ZAP!

There was a bang and a flash – louder and more blinding than before. And then silence.

The silly Billies had vanished, each and every one. The empty swings swung. The empty roundabout ground to a halt.

"Phew!" said Billy.

Silas turned to Billy and hugged him. "Blibba-slibba blobbel!" he cooed.

Chapter Five

Billy was in trouble. Big trouble. Even after he'd delivered Mrs Turbot's leaflets – in one piece this time – and cleaned up all the scraps of paper his double had dropped. Even after he'd washed the gloop off Mr Arkwright's car and polished it till it gleamed. Even after he'd mown Mrs Ramsden's lawn properly . . .

"Never in all my born days," Mr Barnes told him, "have I witnessed such naughty behaviour!"

Billy hung his head. It was pointless trying to explain what had really happened. And anyway, it had been stupid of him to trust the Blobheads. He sighed. Perhaps that was why his double had turned out to be a Silly Billy in the first place.

"You'll be getting no pocket money for the next six weeks," Mr Barnes said.

Billy nodded glumly.

"Not that you'll need it," he went on, "because you're also grounded."

Billy sighed again. It would mean spending more time than ever with the blobby aliens and his talking hamster.

"And if you thought that by carrying out your chores so badly you'd avoid them in future, then you were very much mistaken," his father was saying. "From now on you will help with the washing up, you will vacuum the carpets and wash the kitchen floor every other day. Now go to your room."

Billy turned to go.

"Oh, and another thing," Mr Barnes said. "From now on, you can get your own breakfast."

Billy tried not to smile. *Every cloud*

has a silver lining, he thought as he headed up the stairs. That morning, Mr Barnes had started the day with a kipper and strawberry jam soufflé. Billy would enjoy cornflakes for a change.

"Oh, it's you," said a voice as Billy walked into his bedroom, and the long fluffy purple and red snake in the middle of the floor morphed into Derek.

The inflatable blobby armchair and the doll's house turned back into Kerek and Zerek.

Billy stared at the three Blobheads furiously. "You imbeciles!" he roared.

"Shhh!" hissed Zerek. "I don't want you waking Silas. The High Emperor of the Universe has had a very trying day."

"*He's* had a trying day!" said Billy.
"What about me? You've made things
worse than ever! Now, instead of three
chores to do, I've got dozens."

Derek smiled eagerly. "I can make
you as many helpers as you like," he
said. "Now that the gizmo's working
properly again."

Billy shook his head in disbelief.
"Don't you lot ever learn?" he said.

"There isn't much for hyper-intelligent beings like ourselves *to* learn," said Kerek.

"Right!" Billy snorted. He turned on Derek. "Give me the gizmo. I'm confiscating it."

"I can't," said Derek.

"Come on," Billy persisted. "I know you too well. You'll be using it again the moment my back's turned."

"I won't," said Derek, his blobby head growing redder than usual.

"De-rek!" said Billy, holding out his hand.

Derek hung his head. "I can't find it," he said.

Billy's eyes widened in horror. "Can't find it?" he said. "Are you sure?"

Derek nodded.

"Well, *I* haven't got it," said Kerek.

"Neither have I," said Zerek.

"Where did you lose it?" said Billy. "In the park? On the street?"

"If I knew where I'd lost it then I'd go and find it again," Derek wailed miserably.

"But what if someone else finds it?" said Billy. "What if they play with it. If they press its buttons . . ." He sat down on the corner of the bed and held his head in his hands. "Oh, good grief," he groaned. "This is awful."

"Never mind, Billy," said Kerek, patting him on his shaking shoulders. "It could be worse!"

Billy looked up wearily. "How?" he said.

ZAP! Bang! Flash!

"Yes!" shouted Kevin the hamster triumphantly. "My helpers . . . *fffpllppfffllppff*! Waaah! HELP!"

All eyes turned to the cage in the corner. Fur was sticking out from between every bar, as if a great animal had been stuffed inside. It wasn't one animal though. It was many. Dozens and dozens of identical talking hamsters all crammed together in Kevin's cage. And at the top of the pile, the real Kevin himself – the missing gizmo clutched in his trembling paws.

"Hyper-intelligent beings, I *don't* think!" he squeaked indignantly at the three Blobheads. "I thought you said this thing was working properly now!"

Billy sighed. "And you *believed* them!"

NAUGHTY GNOMES

Chapter One

"Over here, Zerek," Billy called. "On my head!"

Zerek looked puzzled.

"Now!" said Billy.

Zerek shrugged. Then, with a loud cry, he leapt up three metres, landed heavily on Billy's head and wrapped his tentacles tightly round his ears.

"*Unkhh!*" Billy groaned. "What are you doing?"

"You said, 'on my head'," Zerek replied.

"The ball, you fool!" Billy shouted. "Not *you!*"

Kerek trotted over. "But this is *foot*ball," he said. "If you want the ball on your head, it should be called *head*ball!"

"Good point," said Zerek.

"Just give me the ball," Billy sighed.

Zerek picked it up and placed it in Billy's hands. "There," he said.

"*Yuck!*" Billy exclaimed. "It's all wet and slimy! What have you been doing?"

"Dribbling," said Zerek proudly.

"Oh, this is hopeless!" said Billy, dropping the ball and wiping his hands down his jeans. "Blobheads! Honestly!"

Ever since the Blobheads had arrived in Billy's toilet in search of the High Emperor of the Universe, his life had been turned upside down. And as if it wasn't enough that they believed Silas, his baby brother, was that High Emperor; nor that they were now stuck on Earth, perhaps for ever – they were also rubbish at football.

"I thought you were hyper-intelligent beings," said Billy crossly. "I expect this kind of behaviour from Derek, but not from you two." He looked round and frowned. "Where *is* Derek?"

"I sent him to get those tomatoes your father asked you to pick," Kerek explained.

"You did what?" said Billy uneasily.

"Derek's not as sporty as us, you see," Zerek explained.

"And football's far too complicated for him," Kerek added. "So we gave him something simple to do."

"But those tomatoes are important," said Billy. "Dad's cooking a special meal for one of Mum's business clients. Nothing must go wrong!"

"What could go wrong?" said Kerek.

Just then, there came a series of strange noises from beyond the bushes.

Splat! Splat! Splat!

"Wugger-wugger!"

"Ouch!"

"Derek?" Billy shouted and dashed off to where the noises were coming from. Across the lawn, he went, with Kerek and Zerek following close behind. Round the pond. Past the flower beds. Through the arch in the rose-covered trellis. Down the path to the vegetable patch and . . .

Billy froze. His jaw dropped. Six garden gnomes – all with thick white beards and pointy red hats – were jumping up and down on the ground, trampling underfoot the pile of tomatoes which lay there.

"Wugger-wugger!" one of them grunted. It bent down, picked up two juicy-looking specimens and hurled them at Billy, who ducked. The tomatoes splatted on Kerek and Zerek's blobby heads.

"DEREK!" they all bellowed.

At once, a third blobby head popped up from behind the rhubarb, grinning from listening-blob to listening-blob. "Ah, Billy!" said Derek. "Nearly done."

"Nearly done!" Billy shouted. "What's going on? What have you done to my dad's garden gnomes?"

Derek looked at the six gnomes affectionately. "They're my little helpers," he said. "Aren't they sweet . . . *Oof*!" he gasped, as a big, ripe tomato splatted against his own blobby head.

"You've been using your mental tentacle again, haven't you?" said Kerek.

"And how many times have we told you not to?" Zerek added furiously.

Billy shuddered. The last time

Derek had used his mental tentacle, he'd animated all the electrical appliances in the kitchen – and with disastrous consequences. Now he'd brought his dad's six garden gnomes to life. Billy knew that it could only spell trouble.

"I was very careful," Derek was saying. "And they're so cute . . ."

"But my dad's tomatoes!" Billy wailed. "His meal . . ."

"Never fear, Billy," said Derek. "Your tomatoes are safe. I took the precaution of hiding them away." He ducked down behind the rhubarb and emerged a moment later clutching half a dozen tomato plants in each of his upraised tentacles. "*Ta-da*!" he announced. "My little helpers got rid of all those silly red things." He smacked his lips and nibbled at a leaf.

"I must say, this stuff really is delicious!"

"Derek!" Billy shouted. "It's the red things that you eat, not the leaves!" He turned to the gnomes, who were still stomping about in the squelchy heap of squashed tomatoes. "STOP IT!" he roared. "RIGHT NOW!"

The gnomes went quiet and glared at him darkly from beneath heavy eyebrows. Then the largest one stuck two fingers in its mouth and whistled. As one, the six gnomes turned and stomped off into the bushes.

"Now look what you've done!" said Derek. "You've hurt their feelings."

"They were solid concrete," Billy grumbled. "They didn't have feelings before you got hold of them." He glared at Derek. "You've ruined everything!"

Kerek stepped forwards. "This is my fault," he said. "I should have known that even picking tomatoes would prove too difficult for Derek. But calm yourself, Billy. We'll grow some more."

"Grow some more?" said Billy incredulously. "But my dad's due back from the shops any minute."

Kerek smiled, and pulled a small bottle of dark green liquid from a pouch in his belt. "You've obviously never tried Blobby-Grow!" he said. "One drop of this stuff and—"

"Blob's your uncle!" Derek interrupted gleefully.

Kerek bent down, pushed a single tomato pip into the ground with the tip of one tentacle, removed the stopper from the bottle and tipped it up.

Drip! Drip!

Instantly, a thick shoot rose up from the ground, unfurled and grew taller. Small yellow blossoms opened and dropped. In their place tiny green tomatoes appeared, which grew bigger and redder with every passing second.

Billy's eyes grew wide. "This is amazing!" he said.

"I told you," said Kerek, looking up

at the towering plant, laden with ripe tomatoes.

"Are you sure they're all right?" said Billy suspiciously.

"Of course," said Kerek. "They are the finest tomatoes to be found anywhere on Earth."

Derek seized one and sniffed it. "I still think the leaves taste better."

"Leave them alone, Derek!" said Zerek sternly.

"They certainly look all right," said Billy. "OK then, help me to pick some."

With their arms and tentacles balanced full of tomatoes, Billy and the three Blobheads headed for the kitchen. They went up the path, through the rose-covered archway, past the flower beds, round the pond and back across the lawn.

They didn't see the rose bush winding a long thorny creeper around the bird-table, nor hear the ominous rustle of the grass . . .

Chapter Two

Billy peered in through the back door. The kitchen was empty. His parents and Silas were still at the shops.

"Right, you lot," he said. "Follow me. Put your tomatoes on the side over there, and be careful not to squash any."

The Blobheads did as they were told.

"Mission accomplished," said Kerek happily. "Let's go and practise some more dribbling."

"On my head!" Zerek called.

"Football?" said Billy. "Aren't you forgetting something? Derek's *little helpers* are still out there somewhere. We've got to find them and put them back round the pond."

"Billy's right," Kerek sighed. "We can't have a gang of garden gnomes roaming round the garden, throwing tomatoes at the High Emperor!"

"Waaah!" shrieked Zerek in alarm, the blobs on his head flashing red and purple. "Catch those gnomes!"

"And quickly," said Billy urgently. "Before my dad gets back and sees they're missing. He loves those gnomes. He's even given them names . . ."

"You see the trouble you've caused, Derek?" Kerek shouted at Derek. "It's always the same!"

"But the gnomes don't mean any harm," said Derek, peering out of the window. "Poor little things. They must be lonely out there all on their own."

"Don't be so soppy!" snapped Zerek. "And hurry up!"

Armed with a ball of string, a black bin-liner and a fishing net, they set off back across the lawn. The whispery rustling grew louder.

Zerek tripped and tumbled to the ground.

"You should tell your father to mow the lawn," he grumbled.

Billy frowned. The grass was certainly much longer than usual. And he'd never seen geraniums so big. They passed through the arch in the rose-covered trellis.

"Mmm, these roses are delicious," said Derek, stuffing a tentacleful of petals into his mouth. "I— *wurgh!*"

"Derek! Leave that plant alone!" said Kerek sharply as Derek abruptly disappeared into the bush.

"I would do!" Derek gasped, struggling to break free. "But it doesn't seem to want to leave *me* alone! *Ouch!* Those thorns hurt!"

Kerek and Zerek leapt to his aid. They pulled the rose-creepers off him and helped him up.

Billy turned to go on – and stopped in his tracks.

All around him was a mass of tangled vegetation. Giant dandelions and buttercups, and thistles with spikes the size of knitting-needles, towered above him.

"Wh . . . what's going on?" he said.

"*Oops,*" said Kerek.

"What?" said Billy.

"I think we used a little too much Blobby-Grow," he said.

"You can say that again!" said Billy.

"I said, I think we used a little too much—" Kerek began.

"I *heard* what you said!" said Billy.

"But you told me to say it again," said Kerek.

Billy rolled his eyes. "You've turned the garden into a jungle!" he shouted.

"You wanted the tomatoes quickly," Kerek reminded him. "So I used *two* drops rather than one!" He sighed. "The trouble is, Blobby-Grow is designed for the planet Blob, where hardly anything grows."

"It has to be strong to make our blue blobcumbers grow," added Zerek.

"Your Earth gardens are much more unpredictable," Kerek went on. "I didn't realize it would work so well – or spread so far."

"Didn't realize?" Billy spluttered.

"But don't worry, Billy," said Kerek, searching his utility-belt and rummaging through his pockets. "A small amount of Blobby-Shrivel will put it right."

"It'd better," said Billy. "Look at those rose-hips. They're already the size of footballs!"

"On my head!" said Zerek.

Billy scowled at him. "This is no time for—"

SPLAT!

"Hey!" Zerek cried, as the squashed tomato slid down his face. "I wasn't ready."

"It wasn't me," said Derek.

"Or me," said Kerek.

"Then who was it?" said Billy.

From the shadows came a menacing chorus of voices. "Wugger-wugger. Wugger-wugger . . ."

"What wonderful tomatoes!" said Mr Barnes as he put his shopping bags down on the kitchen floor. "My stuffed tomato bake will be a triumph. I'd better get started."

Mrs Barnes tutted impatiently. "I don't know why you always leave everything till the last minute."

"It's all under control," said Mr Barnes. "I've just got to get the mustard and marmalade sauce on . . ."

Mrs Barnes winced. "I'd better put Silas to bed," she said. "Where's Billy?"

"Out in the garden playing football

if I know him," said Mr Barnes. "I'll leave him for now." He strode over to the fridge. "Now where are those sardines?"

"I've had enough of this," said Billy. "Find that Blobby-Shrivel, Kerek. We've got to catch those gnomes. And we can't do that until you've stopped the garden growing."

"I know but . . . I can't seem to find it," said Kerek shamefacedly. "I'm sure it's here somewhere."

"Wugger-wugger! Wugger-wugger!" The sound was coming from their left.

Billy spun round and caught sight of two – three – four pointy hats darting off behind a gigantic begonia.

"There they are!" he yelled, and dashed forwards.

Kerek was behind him, net swishing. Zerek followed, string at the ready. While Derek brought up the rear with the black bin-liner.

"Wugger-wugger!" grunted the gnomes. They ducked down.

"This way!" shouted Billy.

All at once, two hairy hands emerged from the foliage behind him. They seized Kerek's net by the handle and vanished again. There was a loud *crack*, and the two halves of the broken net were tossed back at them.

"You've frightened him!" Derek complained. "Poor little gnomey-womey. Come to Derek." He reached into the shadowy bushes with a tentacle and . . . "OUCH!" he screamed. "He bit me!"

Three more tomatoes sailed out from the dense undergrowth. *Splat!*

Splat! Splat! Followed by a couple more from behind.

Billy turned to see one of the gnomes standing there. He stared at its pointy hat, its glinty teeth, its bushy beard, its beady eyes – at the fishing rod it was brandishing in its hairy hands.

"Uh-oh," said Billy.

There was a rustle to his left, and a second gnome appeared. This one was wielding a little pickaxe. Then a third with a small shovel. A fourth with a miniature garden rake. And a fifth, beating on its wheelbarrow with a tiny trowel.

Billy swallowed nervously.

Finally, the fiercest gnome of all appeared. It tapped a little nobbly walking stick in its hand threateningly.

"Wugger-wugger," it growled.

"Wugger-wugger!" chorused the rest.

They all took a step forwards.

Billy gasped. "We're surrounded!"

Chapter Three

"Now what?" Zerek shrieked, his blobby head flashing furiously.

"We must stay calm," said Kerek. "According to the Great Computer, garden gnomes can *smell* fear."

"Wugger-wugger!" the gnomes grunted. With their arms around each other's shoulders, they were performing a victory can-can dance in front of the four prisoners they'd tied up to the rose-covered trellis.

"But look at their sharp little teeth,"

Zerek wailed. "Look at their horrible pointy nails."

"Get off!" Kerek shouted as the gnome with the shovel jabbed it into his side.

"And leave me alone!" said Derek, as the rose-creeper wound itself round his neck.

"Do something!" yelled Billy. "NOW!"

"What?" said Kerek.

"I don't know . . ." Billy began. "Yes I do. Morph!" he said. "Morph into something really terrifying!"

Ding-dong.

"Can you get that for me?" called Mr Barnes. "I'm up to my eyes in fish heads."

"OK!" Mrs Barnes called back. She came down the stairs, crossed the hall and opened the front door. "Trevor. Maureen," she said. "Do come in. Let me take your coats. Darling," she called. "The Knightsbridges are here. Do go through. This is my husband, Simon."

Mr Barnes turned and smiled as the two dinner guests entered the kitchen. "I won't shake hands," he said. "I'm just gutting the fish."

"I hear you're an excellent cook," said Mrs Knightsbridge. "Trevor here can't even boil an egg!"

"Unless you like them burnt," said Mr Knightsbridge brightly.

"Actually, *adventurous* was the word I used," said Mrs Barnes with a nervous laugh. "Now let me get you a drink."

But Mrs Knightsbridge had stepped forwards and was inspecting the

155

ingredients in a bowl. "Are those pickled onions?" she said.

Mr Barnes nodded. "For the stuffing. Pickled onions, rice and Turkish delight. The fish goes in later. It's a speciality of mine."

Mrs Knightsbridge nodded weakly.

"About that drink!" said Mrs Barnes.

"Brilliant! That *really* scared them," said Billy sarcastically. "Morph into something terrifying I said – and look at you! A deckchair, a footballer and – surprise, surprise! – a giant, fluffy blue kangaroo!"

"Personally, I've always found deckchairs terrifying," said the deckchair stiffly.

"And I suppose *you're* scared of footballers?" Billy said to Kerek.

Kerek shook his head. "Sorry," he

said. "I wasn't concentrating. I've got football on the brain."

"And what's your excuse, Derek?" said Billy.

"He hasn't got one," said the deck-chair sharply. "He *never* concentrates!"

Billy raised his eyebrows impatiently. "I suppose it's up to me to get us out of here," he said, and began struggling furiously. Suddenly the string broke. Quietly disentangling himself, Billy nudged the deckchair next to him. Kerek and Zerek silently morphed back, and tapped the kangaroo on the shoulder. Concentrating hard on their ungainly dance, the gnomes didn't notice a thing.

"Wugger-wugger!"

"Have you got a plan?" Zerek whispered to Billy nervously.

"Yes," Billy shouted. "RUN!"

Mr and Mrs Knightsbridge were at the table waiting for their meal. They looked nervous.

"More wine?" said Mrs Barnes brightly.

"No . . . I . . ." Mr Knightsbridge said. "It's—"

"I made it myself," Mr Barnes called from over by the oven. "Dandelion and nettle, 1995. A vintage year."

"Would you like some, Maureen?" asked Mrs Barnes.

"I'll stick to water, thanks, Alison. I'm driving," she added.

Mr Knightsbridge looked up. "But we came by taxi ... *Ouch*!" he grimaced, as the tip of his wife's right shoe slammed into his shin.

At that moment, Mr Barnes appeared in the doorway with four laden plates balanced up the length of his arm. He strode up to the table and set them down.

"Stuffed Tomato Bake with Mustard and Marmalade Sauce!" he announced proudly. "I think you're going to enjoy this!"

Mrs Knightsbridge poked around in the tomatoes suspiciously. "You weren't joking about the pickled onions," she said.

"They're the key ingredient," said Mr Barnes.

Mr Knightsbridge sliced off a minute morsel of tomato and popped it into his mouth. "Interesting," he said. "But not bad. Delicious tomatoes. Where do you get them?"

"I grow them myself," said Mr Barnes. "I think it's best, don't you? None of those nasty additives!"

Chapter Four

"Do you still think they're sweet and loveable, Derek?" Billy whispered. "Your little gnomey friends."

"I don't understand," said the kangaroo. "They seemed such jolly little chaps. And all that lovely dancing . . ."

Kerek crawled out from beneath the giant daisy they were all hiding under, and peered into the tall, dense vegetation. "I don't know where we are," he said, "but I think we've lost them."

"Thank Blob for that!" muttered Zerek.

"And more good news!" Kerek announced. "I've found the Blobby-Shrivel. It was underneath my memory-gizmo all the time."

"Then use it," said Billy. "Those gnomes could reappear at any moment."

Emerging from their hiding-place, Zerek and Billy watched Kerek remove the stopper from the bottle in his tentacle. It was identical to the bottle of Blobby-Grow, except the liquid inside was brown, not green.

"One . . . two . . ." Kerek said, as he let two drops fall to the ground. "And one for luck!"

Billy watched and waited. And waited and waited . . . "Nothing's happening!" he said impatiently.

"Give it some time," said Kerek.

The sound of grunting came from the bushes. "Wugger-wugger!"

"But we haven't got any time!" said Billy. "We must— Derek, what are you doing?"

Kerek and Zerek turned round to see the giant fluffy blue kangaroo jumping up and down on the spot, higher and higher. "Trying to see where we are," he panted. "I can . . . see a light . . ." He thrust out a fluffy blue paw. "Over there! I think it's the kitchen!"

"Come on, then!" said Billy. "What are we waiting for?"

The Blobheads didn't need telling twice. None of them liked being separated from the High Emperor for so long – particularly with the band of wild gnomes running free. And as

Derek continued to bounce up and down, guiding them on, Kerek and Zerek used their tentacles to hack and slash their way through the overgrown garden.

Behind them, the *wugger-wugger* of the gnomes faded away. From in front, they heard the sound of loud voices and raucous laughter.

"The dinner party seems to be going well," said Billy, relieved. "Dad's tomato dish must have been a hit after all."

When they arrived at the back door, Billy paused and turned to the Blobheads. "If you're coming in, you'd better morph," he said. "And *try* to make it something sensible, Derek," he added to the blue kangaroo.

Then, leaving the three Blobheads to concentrate on their morphing, Billy grasped the door handle and went in.

"That was absolutely delicious," said Mr Knightsbridge, clutching his empty plate with both hands and licking it clean.

"Magnificent!" said his wife, trying to pull it away. "Is there any more?"

"I do hope so," said Mrs Barnes. "Simon?"

"I only wish there were," said Mr Barnes. "It was rather good, wasn't it? – even if I say so myself." He glanced round. "Ah, Billy. There you are," he said, sweeping his long fringe from his eyes. "Mr and Mrs Knightsbridge were just saying how much they liked our tomatoes."

"Dad!" said Billy. "Your hair!"

"Oh, I know," Mr Barnes giggled. "I can't do a thing with it."

"No," said Billy anxiously. "It's . . . it's growing."

"Waaah!" yelled Mr Knightsbridge, from beneath huge, bushy eyebrows which were coiling down over his eyes. "Who turned the lights out?"

"I've got this terrible itch," said Mrs Barnes, scratching furiously under her chin.

"Eeeh!" squealed Mrs Knights-

bridge. "You're growing a beard."

"Waaah!" shrieked Mrs Barnes. "So are you!"

"I can't see a thing!" howled Mr Knightsbridge.

"And I look like Father Christmas!" wailed Mrs Knightsbridge.

"Simon, what's going on?" said Mrs Barnes.

"I . . . I . . ." Mr Barnes stared down

in horror at his own hairy palms, unable to speak.

"Oh no," Billy groaned. He might have known the Blobby-Grow would have side effects. "It must be those tomatoes," he said.

"But it can't be," said Mr Barnes. "They're organic. I grew them myself."

Billy gulped. "The thing is, Dad, they're—"

At that moment four tomatoes flew in through the open window and splatted heavily into the four hairy faces of the grown-ups around the table.

Billy spun round to see the gnomes – all six of them – coming in through the window.

"Wugger-wugger!" they grunted and brandished their assortment of

little implements. "Outside bad! Inside good!"

Mr Barnes's jaw dropped as he recognized them. "Fred. Barney. Bert. Felix," he gasped dizzily. "Duncan. Sid . . . It can't be . . ." He rubbed his eyes. "I must be hallucinating. What *was* in those tomatoes? I . . ."

Suddenly, it was all too much for him. He swooned, slipped from his chair and slid onto the floor in a dead faint.

"Simon!" yelled Mrs Barnes. She leapt to her feet – only to trip over her beard and come crashing down beside her husband.

"Aargh!" screamed Mr Knights-bridge, as a second tomato splatted against his face. He ducked down under the table. "Who keeps doing that?"

"Garden gnomes!" yelled Mrs Knightsbridge, as she jumped up onto the sideboard. "Garden gnomes have invaded the kitchen!"

"You're frightening me, Maureen," Mr Knightsbridge whimpered.

"Get off!" shrieked Mrs Barnes as two of the gnomes began tugging ferociously at her beard. Abandoning her husband, she scurried off towards

the safety of the broom cupboard.

Billy stared round in horror. The gnomes were climbing into everything – the oven, the fridge-freezer, the cupboards and drawers; they were on the table and under the sink.

Mrs Knightsbridge knocked an advancing gnome aside, jumped down from the sideboard and joined her husband under the table, where the pair of them clung desperately on to each other.

"I want to go home," she whispered weakly. "Make them go away, Trevor."

But the gnomes had no intention of leaving. "Outside bad! Inside good!" they chanted as they smashed and squished and swung from the lights and skated along the table. Billy stared at them helplessly.

"Help!" he shouted. "HELP!

Chapter Five

With a loud *Bang!* the door flew open, and in bounded the giant fluffy blue kangaroo with two blobby cowboys on its back.

"Nee-hah!" one of them cried, and twirled a lasso round in the air. "Blobheads to the rescue!"

"Let's catch those naughty gnomes!" shouted the other.

"They shall not get to the High Emperor!" yelled the blue kangaroo, leaping to the far end of the room.

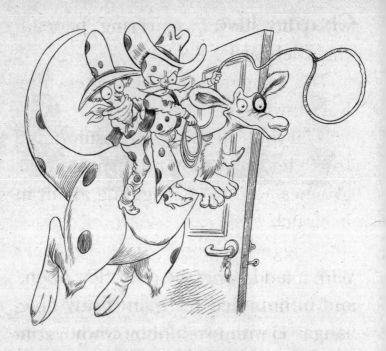

The gnome bouncing up and down
on the chair never stood a chance.
Before it could say "wugger-wugger" it
had been roped, tied and bundled
into Derek's fluffy blue pouch.

A second gnome soon joined it,
followed by a third and a fourth.

"One of them's getting away!" Billy
shouted and pointed at the gnome

with the shovel, scurrying beneath the sideboard.

The kangaroo hopped after him. Kerek swung his lasso.

"Got you!" he cried. He dismounted from the kangaroo and inspected the gnomes, who were wriggling about in its pouch.

"Wugger-wugger!" the gnomes grumbled angrily.

"I think that's all of them," said Kerek. He removed his cowboy hat to reveal the central blob on his head, brightly pulsing with light. "Right!" he announced. "It's time to use our mental tentacles."

"Not *you*, Derek!" Zerek told the kangaroo.

As Billy watched, Kerek and Zerek's mental tentacles fizzed, pulsed and elongated.

"Wugger-wugger!" the gnomes grunted in alarm.

The suckers at the end of the two swaying mental tentacles attached themselves to the gnomes' foreheads one after the other – and, one after the other, the gnomes fell still as they returned to stone.

"There," said Kerek, putting his cowboy hat back into place and turning to Billy. "Happy now?"

"Happy?" said Billy. "Happy! Look at the state of this place!"

The Blobheads looked round. "Nothing that can't be tidied," said Zerek.

"And what about my mum and dad?" said Billy. "And Mr and Mrs Knightsbridge?"

Mr Barnes was out cold on the carpet. Mrs Barnes was missing, presumed hiding in the broom cupboard. While the Knightsbridges – covered from head to toe in thick hair – were still under the table, clinging to one another miserably.

"Blobby-Shrivel," said Kerek. "It's the only answer."

"But the Blobby-Shrivel didn't

work," said Billy. "And anyway, how would you know the right amount to give them?"

"A whiff of the stuff will be enough," said Kerek, pulling the bottle from his belt. "Trust me." He crouched down next to Mr Barnes.

Billy saw his dad's eyes flicker open and dart wildly around the room. "Waaah!" he shrieked. "Cowboy! Kangaroo! Gnomes—"

Kerek unstoppered the bottle and held it under Mr Barnes's nose.

Mr Barnes winced, smiled – and fell back to sleep.

"He'll be fine when he wakes up," Kerek assured him.

"And he won't remember a thing," said Zerek.

"Look," said the blue kangaroo. "His hair's already going."

To his surprise, Billy saw that Derek was right.

With each passing second, the matted tangle of hair – on his dad's head, his face and sprouting from the front of his shirt – was coiling back on itself and disappearing.

"The others!" shouted Zerek. "We must do the others at once."

First Mrs Knightsbridge was given a whiff of the Blobby-Shrivel. Then Mr Knightsbridge. And finally, Mrs Barnes – who Kerek indeed found in the broom cupboard, curled up in a tight ball.

"Let's get them back to their places," said Kerek. "They'll come round when their hair has returned to normal."

By the time they were all seated, fast asleep, at the table again, Mr Barnes

looked almost back to his old self. And apart from the stubble around her cheeks, Mrs Knightsbridge seemed as good as new.

"Billy!" said Kerek. "Stop gawping. You've still got to tidy up."

"Can't you lot help?" said Billy.

"Derek and I can't," said Kerek. "We have to put the garden gnomes back where they belong."

And so saying, he and the giant kangaroo hurried off.

Billy turned to Zerek. "And you?"

"WAAAAH!" came a long, loud wail from above their heads.

It was Silas, awake and frightened by all the noise.

"I must attend to the High Emperor at once," said Zerek, and rushed away to do just that.

"Typical," Billy muttered.

The next minute he was dashing here and there, righting what could be righted and throwing away anything broken beyond repair. He shut the cupboards. He closed the drawers. He wiped the walls, swept the floor and was just about to see to the mess around the fridge when he heard his dad stir.

"Ah, Billy," he said. "There you are. Finished playing football?"

"Y . . . yes, Dad," said Billy. "So far, so good," he thought.

Even though his dad looked a bit groggy, he didn't seem to remember anything that had happened. Neither did the others.

"That was lovely," said Mrs Knightsbridge, patting her lips with a napkin. "Wasn't it, dear?"

"Errm . . . yes," said Mr Knights-bridge, staring down at his spotless plate with some surprise.

Mr Barnes smiled at his wife warmly. "Coffee anyone?" he asked. "After-dinner mints?"

The following morning, Billy was up, dressed and downstairs by six o'clock. Not only was he starving hungry, having missed tea the previous evening, but he also wanted to make sure that every last trace of the splatted tomatoes was gone before his parents got up.

An hour later as he was just wringing out the mop for the final time, the back door opened and Kerek, Zerek and Derek – Blobheads once more – scuttled into the kitchen.

"Trust you to arrive just when all the work's done," said Billy. "But never mind. Do you want to play football now?"

"Football?" said Kerek. "I don't think so."

"I don't really feel like it either," said Zerek.

"Well, let's go into the garden anyway," said Billy. "I could teach you cricket. Or baseball—"

"You want to go into the garden?" said Kerek uneasily.

Billy's eyes narrowed suspiciously. He strode across the kitchen and looked through the window. "Oh no," he gasped. "Oh *no*!"

The Blobby-Shrivel had finally taken effect. Everything – from the giant daisies and dense grass to the geraniums, begonias and roses – had wilted. The garden, covered in a mess of shrivelled vegetation, looked like a huge compost heap.

"I thought it would all go back to normal," said Billy. "Like the hair."

"So did I," admitted Kerek. "But all is not lost. I'm sure the Great Computer will come up with a solution. And look, the gnomes are back in place."

Billy stared glumly at the garden gnomes standing in a cluster around the pond. There was Fred with his wheelbarrow. And Bert with his shovel. And Felix. And Duncan. And Sid . . .

"Barney!" Billy exclaimed.

"Pardon?" said Zerek.

"There should be six gnomes," said Billy. "Not five. Barney's missing!"

Just then, a loud scratching noise erupted from behind the skirting board. Billy froze. The Blobheads' red and purple blobs pulsed. As one, they all turned their heads, following the noise as it scuttled along the inside of the wall, up to the ceiling and back above their heads.

"What is it?" Billy gasped. "A mouse? A rat?"

Abruptly, the sound of movement stopped and a grunting noise echoed through the cavity walls. "Wugger-wugger!"

"A garden gnome!" Billy exclaimed.
"Actually," said Kerek. "I think you'll
find he's a *house* gnome now . . ."

PURPLE ALERT!

Chapter One

Zerek rushed into Billy's bedroom, the blobs on his head fizzing alarmingly.

"Purple alert!" he shouted. "Purple alert!"

"What is it now?" said Billy wearily, looking up from his comic. "Don't tell me. Derek's morphed into a giant fluffy blue kangaroo and got his head stuck in the banisters again."

"I haven't," said Derek indignantly from the corner of the room.

"No, he's probably spotted that garden gnome you let in," said Kevin the talking hamster. "Horrible little thing. It should be kept in a cage," he added, rattling the bars of his own cage.

"No, it's nothing like that," said Zerek.

"Then explain yourself," said Kerek.

"It's the Great Computer," said Zerek. "Look!"

"*Pfffff*!" said Billy. "That heap of junk can't get anything right. It brought you halfway across the galaxy. It told you my baby brother Silas was the High Emperor of the Universe . . ."

But the Blobheads weren't listening. They clustered round the flashing, bleeping screen, their blobby heads pulsing brightly.

"The Wormhole Alarm!" said Kerek.

"Precisely!" said Zerek.

"It's coming!" Derek shouted excitedly.

"What is?" said Billy.

"A wormhole!" said Zerek impatiently.

Billy frowned. "Wasn't that how you got here in the first place?"

"Indeed!" said Kerek. "It is the portal between two points in space, enabling one to traverse the universe in the blink of an eye."

"What?" said Billy.

"It's like a doorway between here and there," said Derek.

"It can appear from nowhere," added Kerek. "And in the least likely places."

"Oh, yes," said Billy. "If I remember rightly, it appeared in the toilet the first time."

Zerek shuddered. "Yes, and I for one don't want to go back down the toilet. Not now I know what you humans use it for."

"The wormhole never appears in exactly the same place twice," said Kerek. "The Great Computer will tell us where it will materialize this time."

"Remain on purple alert everyone!" said Zerek. "Purple Alert! Purple—"

Abruptly, the flashing and bleeping ceased.

"It's stopped," said Billy.

"Yes," said Kerek. "It seems there was no wormhole after all."

"Don't tell me the Great Computer got it wrong," said Billy sarcastically.

"The Great Computer is never wrong," said Kerek. "Though some-times it can become a little confused."

Billy snorted. "So it wasn't really a purple alert," he said.

"It was purple-ish," said Zerek sheepishly.

"In fact it wasn't an alert at all," said Billy. "Was it?"

"I—" Zerek began.

"You should be careful," Billy went on. "One day you'll call Purple Alert and no one will believe you."

"Like that story," said Derek

brightly. "*The Boy Who Cried Woof!*"

"Wolf!" Billy corrected him.

"*Waaah*!" the Blobheads all cried out with alarm. "Where?"

"The story," said Billy. "It's called—"

"Billy!" his dad shouted from downstairs. "Are you ready?"

"Ready?" Billy shouted back. "What for?"

"We're going to the supermarket," his dad replied. "Don't you remember? I'm cooking a special meal for Mum when she gets back from that sales conference."

A sinister growl came from behind the skirting board. "Wugger-wugger!" It was the garden gnome that Derek had brought to life.

Billy raised his eyes to the ceiling. "Blobheads!" he complained. "Who'd have them? They teach my hamster to talk. They infest the house with gnomes . . ."

"Hurry up, Billy," called his dad. "Silas and I are waiting."

Billy got up. "Coming, Dad!"

"Wugger-wugger!"

"Yes, let's go," said Zerek.

"You?" said Billy. "*You're* not going anywhere. None of you are."

"Oh, please, Billy," the Blobheads pleaded. "You can't leave us here with that gnome on the loose."

"Honestly!" Kevin piped up. "Big Blobheads like you, afraid of a little garden gnome. You should be ashamed of yourselves."

"It's all right for you in your cage," said Derek. "You've got your bars to protect you."

"Don't remind me," said Kevin glumly. "Of course," he added, "you could always let me out. I'm not scared of garden gnomes."

"Don't even *think* of letting him out, Derek!" said Billy.

"I wasn't!" said Derek. "I wouldn't . . . Only, please take us with you."

"No!" said Billy.

"Wugger-wugger!"

"We would consider it a great kindness!" said Kerek.

"You know how fierce gnomes can be," said Zerek. "With their sharp little teeth and horrid pointy nails." He shuddered nervously.

"Go on, Billy!" said Derek. "Be a spot!"

"Absolutely not!" said Billy. "And that's final!"

Chapter Two

Fifteen minutes later, Billy was waiting in the car which was parked outside the Megasaver Supermarket. His dad was off with Silas, looking for a trolley with a seat.

"You won't regret this," said the blobby scarf round his neck.

"Not for a moment," added the blobby jacket.

"You won't even notice we're here," said the hat.

Billy glanced up at the huge, blobby

bowler hat Derek had morphed into and groaned. "How do I let myself get talked into these things?" he muttered.

Just then, his dad returned pushing a trolley. "Come on, Billy," he said.

"And behave yourselves, you lot!" Billy hissed, as he climbed out of the car.

"We will," said the Blobheads.

"As good as goldfish," said the hat.

"Pardon, Billy?" said his dad, turning round. He frowned. "And what's that on your head?"

"This?" said Billy uneasily. "Everyone's wearing them. They're well cool."

"Well, I think it looks ridiculous," he said.

Silas pointed at the hat. "Blobbolobbel!" he gurgled happily.

"And so does Silas!" said his dad, and marched off.

"He doesn't," said the hat indignantly. "Do you, High Emperor?"

"Stop arguing, Billy," his dad shouted back. "Let's just do our shopping and go before anyone we know sees you looking like that."

For once, Billy agreed with his dad. The sooner he got the three

Blobheads back home, the better.

As they approached the main entrance – with Mr Barnes in front, pushing Silas in the shopping trolley and Billy, still wearing the three disguised Blobheads, following behind – the doors slid open. The air filled with the sound of terrible plinky-plinky music.

> *My, my, my!*
> *I love your eyes!*
> *Yeah, yeah, yeah!*
> *I love your hair!*

Billy felt the scarf tremble.

"This music," said the jacket dramatically. "I don't like it one little bit."

"Neither do I, Zerek," Billy whispered back. "But it's only one of Smooch's greatest hits."

"One of evil Sandra's favourite tunes," said the scarf ominously, and tightened its grip round his neck.

"*Wurrgh!*" gasped Billy, struggling to loosen it. "Get off, Kerek. And stop that nonsense about evil Sandra."

Ever since that fateful day when the Blobheads had first arrived, they'd gone on and on about evil Sandra and her wicked followers. They were evil aliens, Kerek claimed, who had come to earth to abduct the High Emperor of the Universe. What was worse, they were now convinced that this evil Sandra was his and Silas's babysitter, Sandra Smethwick. And there was nothing Billy could say to persuade them otherwise.

"May I help you, sir?" came a voice. "Our aim is to make your shopping experience a happy one."

Billy looked up to see a thin, spotty youth with a price gun smiling at his dad. His name – *Roy* – was on a badge pinned to the lapel of his green jacket.

"*Errm*, let me see," said Mr Barnes. "I'm looking for prunes and, ah yes, mustard."

"Please find prunes in aisle 7," said Roy brightly. "And mustard in aisle 9."

"Thank you," said Mr Barnes.

"Thank *you,* sir," said Roy.

"Creep," Billy muttered as he followed his dad away.

"Creepy behaviour indeed," said the scarf.

"Wicked-Follower-of-Sandra behaviour," added the jacket.

"Oh, be quiet!" Billy snapped.

They found the prunes, and the mustard. Mr Barnes inspected his list. "Now where do you think they keep the tripe?"

"In the CD player, by the sound of it," said Billy.

"Tripe?" came a voice behind them. Billy turned to see a pale, plump girl with red hair and freckles. She was busy stacking cans of tuna. "All stomach lining is kept in the offal cooler, aisle 4," she said, "along with the livers, kidneys, hearts and tongues."

"*Waaah!*" shrieked the hat.

Mr Barnes glared at Billy. "There's nothing wrong with tripe," he snapped. "Thanks," he said, turning back to the girl. She smiled and pointed at her name badge. "Thanks, *Tanya,*" he said.

"Thank *you*, sir," said Tanya. "Our aim is to make your shopping experience a happy one." Her gaze fell on Silas. "Oh, what a gorgeous baby. What's his name?"

"Silas," said Mr Barnes.

"How lovely!" She stepped forwards and tickled Silas under his chin. "Coochie-coochie!"

"*Pfoooah!*" Billy gasped as he was struck by a blast of Tanya's appallingly bad breath. He staggered backwards, eyes watering. His jacket zip shot up and down agitatedly.

"It could almost be the breath of evil Sandra itself," whispered the scarf. "And, as the *Book of Krud* reminds us, 'The foulness of their breath and terrible taste in music are matched only by their hatred of sweet smells and soft fluffy things. Be warned! Be warned . . .'"

"Oh, give it a rest!" said Billy.

"Billy, do keep up," his dad called

back to him impatiently. "If I don't get my prune and pigeon pie in the oven soon, it'll never be ready in time."

"Yes, hurry," said the jacket impatiently. "We must not lose sight of the High Emperor."

Urged on by the Blobheads, Billy trotted after his dad and Silas. At the end of the aisle, he skidded round the corner – and ran slap bang into a gangly youth with greasy hair and a big nose who was dressed in supermarket-uniform green.

"*Ouch!*" he squeaked as he tumbled back into the shelves. The feather dusters he'd been stacking tumbled all round him.

"Whoops!" said Billy. "Sorry!"

Mr Barnes spun round. "Do be careful, Billy!" he said. He turned to the youth and glanced at his name badge. "Apologies for my son's clumsy behaviour, Dominic."

"No harm done," the youth replied, climbing to his feet. He began returning the feather dusters gingerly to the shelves.

"You see that," whispered the scarf. "He obviously doesn't like the feel of those soft, fluffy objects."

"Just like Sandra and its wicked

followers," added the jacket.

The hat gulped nervously. "And here come the others."

Billy turned to see Roy and Tanya hurrying towards them.

"Is everything all right?" said Roy. "We heard a crash."

"I'm fine," said Dominic, then shuddered as his hand brushed against one of the feather dusters. "Though you could help me re-stack this lot."

"Hello again," said Tanya, patting Silas's head. "Isn't he gorgeous, Roy? And his name's *Silas*," she added.

Roy and Dominic stopped what they were doing and looked at Silas with interest.

"Silas," they repeated.

Just then, the music was interrupted by a soothing voice informing customers of a special offer at the cheese counter.

"Peruvian blue llama's cheese," said Billy's dad brightly. "That sounds interesting."

"You'll find the cheese counter opposite the end of aisle 8," said Tanya.

"Thank you again," said Billy's dad.

"Thank *you* again, sir," said Tanya.

"Our aim is to make your shopping experience a happy one," she, Roy and Dominic said in unison.

"What nice polite young people," said Billy's dad. "You could learn something from them, Billy."

Billy glanced back. The three shop assistants caught his gaze, turned away and began inspecting a shelf of tinned fruit.

"I think they're following us," the

hat muttered.

"No doubt about it, Derek," said the jacket anxiously.

"Which is precisely what the wicked Followers of Sandra do," said the scarf darkly. "They *follow*."

"Nonsense, Kerek," said Billy. "They're just doing their job." He turned to follow his dad, who was wheeling the trolley towards the far end of the aisle.

At the cheese counter, a girl with a red-and-white striped hat and apron was standing with her back turned. Mr Barnes cleared his throat.

"I wondered if I could sample the Peruvian blue llama cheese," he said. The assistant turned, a broad smile on her face. It was Sandra. The babysitter.

"I didn't know you worked here," said Mr Barnes.

"Only at weekends," she said. "Hello, Silas."

Billy rounded the corner of aisle 9, and stopped.

"Look," he said. "It's Sandra Smethwick."

"WAAAH!" screamed the Blobheads. "Purple Alert! Purple Alert!"

Chapter Three

"Don't be ridiculous!" said Billy. "It's just our babysitter."

But the Blobheads weren't listening. The hat went right down over Billy's face. The jacket pulled him backwards. The scarf tightened round his neck and tugged him away.

"*Mffll blwchh!*" Billy mumbled as he staggered blindly back into aisle 9.

"You don't understand," said the scarf. "It's the evil Sandra."

"We must be in its headquarters," said the hat.

"I *knew* they were its followers! And they're all around us," said the jacket with a sweep of its blobby sleeves.

"They're everywhere!" howled the scarf.

"Nonsense!" Billy gasped. "Y . . . you're strangling me!"

Just then, Tanya and Roy appeared. "Can we help you?" they asked.

"No . . . I . . ." Billy began.

"I think we *can*," said Tanya. "Don't you, Roy?"

"I certainly do," came the reply and, before Billy had a chance to object, the two shop assistants removed his hat, jacket and scarf.

"We'll put these in our special cloakroom," said Tanya.

"But—"

"Don't worry, sir," said Roy. "It's all part of the service."

"We don't want you getting all hot and bothered," said Tanya.

"Our aim is to make your shopping experience a happy one," they chorused, scurrying away with the three disguised Blobheads clasped tightly in their hands.

Billy ran after them. "No, wait! Stop!" he cried. "You don't understand!"

"Billy, is that you making all that noise?" It was his dad. "And where's that ridiculous hat you were wearing? And your jacket and scarf . . . Don't tell me you've lost them!"

"No, Dad," said Billy. He pointed at Roy and Tanya. "*They've* got them. They're taking them to the cloak-room."

"Oh, well, that's all right then," said

Billy's dad. "Come and try this cheese. It's absolutely delicious."

Reluctantly, Billy followed his dad to the counter. Sandra held out a cube of blue cheese on a fork. Billy winced.

"It stinks!" he said.

"Rubbish," said his dad. "It's . . . Actually, it *is* a bit whiffy."

Sandra smiled. "I don't think it's the cheese at all," she said. "I think it's little Silas." She turned to him. "Someone's done a little something in his nappy."

"Oh, dear," said Mr Barnes. "I'd better change it."

"Don't you worry about that," said Sandra, coming round the counter. "I'll change him. It's all part of the service. Our aim is to make your shopping experience a happy one."

And with that, she grabbed Silas

from the shopping trolley and whisked him away. Billy's dad watched them disappearing through a side door.

"Aren't they considerate here?" he said to Billy. "Now, are you sure you won't try this cheese?"

"No thanks, Dad," said Billy. "I must get my clothes back."

And before his dad could say

anything, he dashed off to find the Blobheads.

Billy scoured the aisles. Tanya and Roy were nowhere to be seen. Then, just as he was about to give up, he saw the pair of them emerging from a door marked *Strictly Private*. Billy ran over to them.

"My hat, jacket and scarf," he said breathlessly. "I want them back."

"What hat, jacket and scarf is that?" said Tanya.

"The ones you just took off me," said Billy.

"I think sir's mistaken," said Tanya. "Have you seen sir's hat, jacket and scarf, Roy?"

Roy shook his head.

"No, I'm sure we'd have remembered. Our aim is to make your

shopping experience a happy one. We'd have remembered, wouldn't we, Roy?"

"Oh, yes," said Roy, smiling. "We'd have remembered."

"But you *did* take them!" said Billy. He looked around helplessly. "I want to speak to the manager!"

"Manager?" said Roy. "I don't think we have one of those, do we, Tanya?"

"You'll have to speak to Sandra," said Tanya.

"Sandra?" Billy exclaimed. "My babysitter?"

Just then, he heard muffled voices from behind the door.

"They're in there!" said Billy. "I can hear them!"

"We didn't hear anything, did we, Roy?" said Tanya, a smile playing round her mouth.

"No," said Roy. "Our aim is to—"

"Yes, yes," said Billy. "If you want to make my shopping experience a happy one, then let me get my hat, jacket and scarf." And with that, he barged his way between the plump girl and pimply youth and seized the door handle. The next instant two pairs of exceptionally strong hands grabbed him by the arms and lifted him into the air.

"You don't want to go in there," said Roy calmly.

"It's just a boring old stock cupboard," Tanya added sweetly.

"Put me down!" Billy demanded.

Tanya and Roy glanced at one another, nodded, and released their grip. Billy tumbled to the floor with a bump.

"Our aim is to make your shopping

experience a happy one," they trilled.

Billy picked himself up and backed away. Something was definitely not right. He thought of the Blobheads, and everything they'd told him about Sandra and her wicked followers. Then, looking round, he caught sight of the shelf of fluffy feather dusters which Dominic had finished stacking.

"Maybe I'm crazy," Billy muttered. "But . . ."

He raced across, seized two of the feather dusters and advanced towards Tanya and Roy. There was an unmistakable glint of fear in their eyes.

"Open the door!" Billy demanded.

"Wh . . . what are you doing with those?" said Tanya.

"Open the door!" said Billy, louder.

"Put them down," said Roy. "There's a good customer."

But Billy did not put them down. Instead, he reached forwards with the feather dusters. He tickled Tanya under one arm. He tickled Roy beneath his spotty chin.

"*Waaah! Ouch!*" they shrieked, and ran away. "Sandra!" Billy heard them howl. "We've got another awkward customer!"

Billy stared at the feather dusters in

surprise. It was certainly weird, but
they'd worked. At that moment the
muffled voices cried out again.

"Let us out!"

"I'm coming," said Billy. He grasped
the handle, pushed the door open –
and dropped one of the feather
dusters in surprise. "*What*?!" he
gasped.

Chapter Four

Instead of a stock cupboard, Billy found himself staring into a vast hangar. Lights flashed, machines beeped, while the music – Snogadelic's latest hit single – was deafening. Several of the green-uniformed shop assistants were pushing full shopping trolleys this way and that in time to the stodgy beat.

Billy stepped forwards and gawped at a curious object standing in the shadows at the very end of the hall. He couldn't believe his eyes. It was a gigantic discus-shaped object perched upon tripod-legs. Its green, warty outer-casing oozed and dripped . . .

"Will you get us out of here!" came an impatient voice.

Billy turned round and there – locked inside a cage labelled *Awkward Customers* – were Kerek, Zerek and Derek, Blobheads once more. And they were not the only ones there. An old woman in a lime-green hat and overcoat stood to their left; a young man in a suit to their right.

"Over here!" they were all shouting. "Let us out!"

Billy ran to the cage to find that the door had been secured with a large padlock. It seemed to be made of the same warty, oozy material as the giant discus-shaped object.

"Use the feather duster!" Kerek bellowed.

Billy brushed it against the padlock. The whole lot immediately turned to jelly and fell, with a loud *splat*, to the floor.

The door burst open and everyone tumbled out.

"Thank Blob you came when you did, Billy," said Kerek.

"I only asked about the sell-by date on the fish fingers," said the old woman indignantly. "I shan't shop here again."

"They caught us unawares," said Zerek. He shuddered. "We are in a place of great evil."

"Would you mind turning the music down a bit?" said the man in the suit. "That's all I asked. I mean what kind of a supermarket is this?" He looked at the three Blobheads. "Great costumes, kids, but isn't it a bit early for Halloween?"

"Come on," said the old woman. "I'm going to find the manager!" And the two of them marched off towards the door.

Zerek grabbed Billy by the arms. "Where is the High Emperor?"

"Silas?" said Billy. "Sandra took him

away to change his nappy. That's all."

"WAAAH!" screamed all three Blobheads.

"We must find him!" shouted Kerek, dashing off.

"We must wrest him from the clutches of evil Sandra!" shouted Zerek.

"Blobheads to the rescue!" shouted Derek, as he chased after the others.

Billy found himself standing alone. Behind him, the warty, oozy slime-encrusted object began to emit a dull, throbbing light. A deep rumbling noise drowned out the sound of Snogadelic's warbling harmonies as, far above his head, the roof began to open.

Then, out of the corner of his eye, Billy caught a glimpse of movement. He looked round to see Sandra striding purposefully through a set of swing doors and off towards the far end of the vast room where the object stood.

"There, there," she was cooing. "Now, Silas, you and I are going on a nice little trip."

"Sandra! Silas!" Billy called out, and raced towards them.

"Billy!" said Sandra, surprised. "What are you doing here?"

Billy stopped. Silas giggled and pointed a pudgy finger at him. "Billibel," he said.

Billy smiled nervously. "Hello, Silas," he said. He turned to Sandra. "Thanks for changing his nappy. If you just give him back to me, I'll go and find my dad."

"I don't think so," said Sandra, smiling back sweetly.

Billy reached out for Silas. "Really," he said. "I'll take him now."

"Now, don't be a silly boy," said Sandra. "We don't want any unpleasantness."

"Our aim is to make your shopping experience a happy one," came a chorus of soothing voices.

Billy looked round to see Tanya, Roy and Dominic. He was surrounded.

"Put down that feather duster and

231

step aside," said Sandra. Her face grew hard. "Our spaceship awaits!"

"Spaceship," Billy gasped. He spun round and stared at the discus-shaped object with its pulsing green lights. "But—"

All at once there was an almighty *CRASH*! as the swing doors burst open for a second time and in trundled two heavily laden – and curiously blobby – shopping trolleys. They hurtled across the concrete floor, screeched to an abrupt halt and catapulted their contents up into the air.

Perfume bottles smashed and aerosols exploded. The whole area was drenched in a thousand different scents and fragrances. And as the air cleared, a spectacular array of tissues, fluffy slippers, feather dusters and cotton-wool balls tumbled down

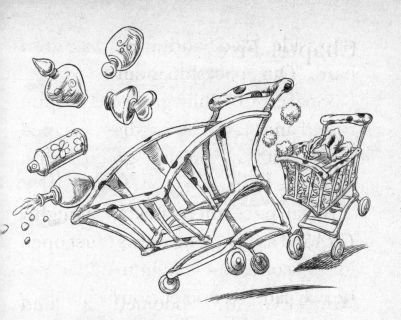

to the ground.

"*Ouch! Ugh! Aaargh!*" shrieked Tanya, Roy and Dominic as they dashed for cover.

"WAAAAH!" screeched Sandra, flinging her arms up in horror.

Silas flew into the air, squealing with delight.

"Silas!" cried Billy.

"High Emperor!" wailed the two shopping trolleys.

Chapter Five

"*GER-ANI-UM*!" boomed a loud voice.

Billy turned to see a giant fluffy blue kangaroo leaping high up into the air after the flying Silas, reach out and catch the small child in his fluffy paws. Silas giggled – and slipped!

"Silas!" Billy screamed.

"High Emperor!" cried the shopping trolleys, morphing back into Kerek and Zerek.

"Gotcha!" said the kangaroo, as Silas dropped down into his pouch.

"Thank goodness!" breathed Billy.

The kangaroo landed back on the ground, retrieved Silas from the pouch and changed back into Derek. "I always knew that morphing into a giant fluffy blue kangaroo would come in handy one day," he said smugly.

"Yes, well done," said Kerek.

"Morph into a shopping trolley, *you* said."

"All right, Derek," said Kerek.

"Load yourself up with aftershave, *you* said."

"Derek! That's enough!" Kerek shouted. "Let's get out of here!"

A voice echoed from the shadows. "Not so fast!" it roared.

It was Sandra. Behind her were Tanya, Roy and Dominic. The four of them stepped closer. Derek hid Silas behind his back.

"So this is the way you want to play, is it?" said Sandra. She laughed unpleasantly. "That's fine by me," she said. "No more nice Sandra!"

With that, she reached up with both hands, grasped the hair at the back of her neck and tugged. Her wig and mask came away. Then, with a loud *rrrrip*! she tore off the rest of her human disguise and tossed it aside. Billy found himself staring at a grotesque pink monster with countless arms and eight glowing eyes.

"S . . . S . . . Sandra," Billy stammered. "You really *are* an evil monster from outer space!"

Tanya, Roy and Dominic raised their arms and tore off their own disguises. They looked just like Sandra – only smaller. "Our aim is to make your shopping experience a happy one," they hissed.

"W . . . what do we do now?" Billy faltered.

"Nothing," said Kerek miserably.

"Our one mission was to protect the High Emperor," said Zerek, "and

we have failed."

"Now Sandra will take over the universe," said Derek tearfully. "And it's all our fault!"

"But . . . it isn't true," said Billy. "It can't be."

"Oh, but it is," said Sandra coldly. It turned to Derek. "Hand him over!" it demanded.

"I . . . I don't know where he is," said Derek.

"Blobber-lobbel," Silas gurgled from behind Derek's back.

"With the High Emperor in my clutches, I shall rule the cosmos!" Sandra roared. "There will be foul odours and sharp pointy things everywhere – and every creature in the universe will dance to plinky-plinky music! Now, give him to ME!"

Bleep! Bleep! Bleep!

"Hey!" said Billy. "The Great Computer . . ."

"It's the Wormhole Alarm," said Kerek dejectedly. "Not that it matters now."

"Purple Alert," said Zerek. "For what it's worth."

"Poor High Emperor," said Derek, patting Silas with a tentacle. "You'd have enjoyed a ride down a worm-hole." He sighed. "Too late now."

"For the last time, hand him over!" rasped Sandra, stretching out its claws. "Give him to—"

It didn't finish its sentence, for at that moment a loud swooshing sound filled the cavernous building as a giant, translucent tube suddenly materialized and – with an extra loud *swoosh* – sucked the evil Sandra into its dark, circular portal.

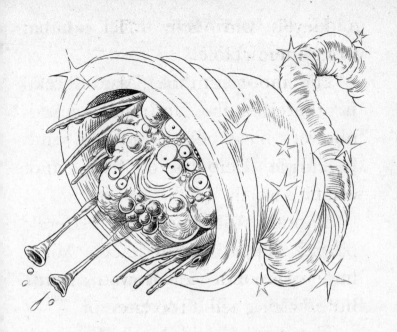

"Sandra! Sandra!" cried its evil followers, rushing after it.

Swoosh Swoosh Swoosh!! Each in turn disappeared. Then, with a loud *POP!* the wormhole itself vanished.

"Where have they all gone?" said Billy.

"They could be anywhere," said Zerek. "Without a Great Computer to guide you, wormhole travel can be very unpredictable."

"The important thing," said Kerek, "is that Sandra and its wicked followers have been banished, and the High Emperor is safe and sound."

"All thanks to me," said Derek.

Zerek stepped forwards. "The High Emperor is indeed safe and sound. But how long will he remain so?"

"That's right," said Derek. "Spoil my moment of triumph."

"Be quiet, Derek," said Kerek. "What do you mean, Zerek?"

"I mean that it is too difficult protecting the High Emperor of the Universe here on Earth," said Zerek. "We need to get him back to Blob where he can be properly looked after." He nodded towards the far end of the hangar. "We have the means."

"Sandra's spaceship," said Kerek. "Of course!"

"No," Billy mumbled as he realized what the Blobheads had in mind. "You can't! You *mustn't!*"

"It's for the best, Billy," said Kerek, as he trotted off towards the spaceship, the others following close behind.

"Come back!" Billy shouted. He raced after them. "Stop! I won't let you—" He stopped, looked down and burst out laughing. "I don't think you'll be going very far in *that!*"

Where the spaceship had stood, a gloopy green mess now covered the floor.

"It was the perfume," said Kerek sadly.

"And the feather dusters," said Zerek.

"They've dissolved the spaceship completely!" said Derek.

Billy turned away. "Come on, you lot," he said. "Morph back. We're going home."

Kerek and Zerek turned back into the scarf and jacket. Derek held Silas out to Billy.

"I think his nappy really does need changing this time," he said, and morphed into a big, blobby jester's hat complete with tassels and bells.

"Fantastic," Billy groaned. He made his way back to the door to the supermarket. "Oh, and by the way, Derek," he said. "When you leap into battle, you shout 'Geronimo!' not 'Geranium!'"

"Nonsense," said the hat. "I know

for a fact that a geronimo's a big red flower with smelly leaves. Why would anyone want to shout that?"

"Sssh!" hissed the jacket. "There's Billy's father."

"There you are, Billy," said Mr Barnes. "You took your time. And goodness knows where Sandra's got to."

"Actually, Dad," said Billy. "I think we might need a new babysitter."

Back in Billy's bedroom that evening, the Blobheads were reliving their moment of triumph.

"We weren't afraid," said Kerek, "not even for a moment."

"We defeated evil Sandra with our brilliant tactics and masterful cunning," said Zerek.

"Brave and fearless, we are," said

Derek. "Nothing scares us—"

"Wugger-wugger!"

"*Waaah!*" screeched the three Blobheads and huddled together.

The grunting noise had come, not from behind the wall, but from the table. Billy and the Blobheads looked round to see the garden gnome sitting beside Kevin's cage, while Kevin

himself was nonchalantly leaning against the open door.

"Honestly!" said Kevin. "Afraid of a garden gnome! He's really rather sweet when you get to know him – and obedient. He let me out of my cage." He paused. "Not at all like this Sandra character by the sound of it."

"Oh, I think we can safely say we've seen the last of evil Sandra," said Derek, puffing out his chest. "Now if you can just persuade the *gnome* to get into the cage and close the door . . ."

Far, far away on the other side of the galaxy, a hideous pink monster dragged itself from a perfumed fluff-pool on the planet Powderpuff and looked round with its eight glowing eyes.

"You haven't seen the last of me yet!" it rasped. "I'll be back! You mark my words. Sandra will return!"

If you enjoyed BLOBHEADS GO BOING!,
look out for

Muddle Earth

by Paul Stewart and Chris Riddell

Where would you find a perfumed bog filled with pink stinky hogs and exploding gas frogs? A place that's home to a wizard with only one spell, an ogre who cries a lot and a very sarcastic budgie. Welcome to Muddle Earth. A place where anything can happen – and it usually does.

Joe Jefferson, an ordinary schoolboy from ordinary earth, is about to find his life changed forever. Prepare for a great battle of good, evil and sort-of OK . . .